A Candlelight Ecstasy Romance®

"I'VE MADE IT CLEAR THAT I WANT YOU," ADAM MURMURED.

"I guess the question is whether or not that's enough for you."

Kim stared at him blankly. "Enough? You mean, will I settle for us sleeping together?"

"I prefer the term 'lovers.'"

"Call it what you like," she seethed. "It all comes down to the same thing. All you're interested in is my body!"

"Actually, you're wrong. I find your devious little mind an endless source of fascination. But I can't deny your body—"

"So you want me to be your mistress. Marriage just isn't what you had in mind. Well, no thanks. I'd find it too painful and compromising. I don't want half a loaf, Adam. I want the whole thing."

CANDLELIGHT ECSTASY CLASSIC ROMANCES

THE TAWNY GOLD MAN, *Amii Lorin*
GENTLE PIRATE, *Jayne Castle*

CANDLELIGHT ECSTASY ROMANCES®

QUANTITY SALES

Most Dell Books are available at special quantity discounts when pur-
chased in bulk by corporations, organizations, and special-interest
groups. Custom imprinting or excerpting can also be done to fit special
needs. For details write: Dell Publishing Co., Inc., 1 Dag Hammarskjold
Plaza, New York, NY 10017, Attn.: Special Sales Dept., or phone: (212)
605-3319.

INDIVIDUAL SALES

Are there any Dell Books you want but cannot find in your local stores? If
so, you can order them directly from us. You can get any Dell book in
print. Simply include the book's title, author, and ISBN number, if you
have it, along with a check or money order (no cash can be accepted) for
the full retail price plus 75¢ per copy to cover shipping and handling.
Mail to: Dell Readers Service, Dept. FM, P.O. Box 1000, Pine Brook,
NJ 07058.

SEDUCTIVE DECEIVER

Kathy Orr

A CANDLELIGHT ECSTASY ROMANCE®

Published by
Dell Publishing Co., Inc.
1 Dag Hammarskjold Plaza
New York, New York 10017

Copyright © 1986 by Kathy Orr

All rights reserved. No part of this book may be reproduced or transmitted in any form or by any means, electronic or mechanical, including photocopying, recording, or by any information storage and retrieval system, without the written permission of the Publisher, except where permitted by law.

Dell ® TM 681510, Dell Publishing Co., Inc.

Candlelight Ecstasy Romance®, 1,203,540, is a registered trademark of Dell Publishing Co., Inc., New York, New York.

ISBN: 0-440-17617-4

Printed in the United States of America

September 1986

10 9 8 7 6 5 4 3 2 1

WFH

To Our Readers:

We have been delighted with your enthusiastic response to Candlelight Ecstasy Romances®, and we thank you for the interest you have shown in this exciting series.

In the upcoming months we will continue to present the distinctive sensuous love stories you have come to expect only from Ecstasy. We look forward to bringing you many more books from your favorite authors and also the very finest work from new authors of contemporary romantic fiction.

As always, we are striving to present the unique, absorbing love stories that you enjoy most—books that are more than ordinary romance. Your suggestions and comments are always welcome. Please write to us at the address below.

Sincerely,

The Editors
Candlelight Romances
1 Dag Hammarskjold Plaza
New York, New York 10017

SEDUCTIVE DECEIVER

CHAPTER ONE

"All rise. This court is now in session, the Honorable Margaret Wilder presiding."

It was the eighteenth of May and quite possibly the second-worst day in Kim Forester's life. The bailiff's words, sonorous with doom, foreshadowed the defeat she feared was about to be handed down to her, and she wished with aching futility that she could go back to her childhood, to the golden years when she and her twin Greg had been invincible, had never thought to question their immortality.

The judge, a woman in her early fifties with smartly styled hair and calm blue eyes, appeared from her chambers, black robes swirling in her wake, and took her seat at the bench. "I have reviewed the evidence in this case," she pronounced as the rustle of bodies subsided, "weighed it carefully, and arrived at a decision concerning custody of the child, Jason Gregory Forester."

Across the room, Adam Ryan sat impassive, no sign of the anxiety that gripped Kim evident in his features. His eyes, gray and hooded, regarded the judge unblinkingly.

"It is tragic when a child loses both parents and must then be put in the position of choosing between his surviving relatives. Since this child is little more than a baby, that choice rests with me and is one to which I have devoted a great deal of thought."

The judge paused impressively, then focused her gaze on Adam. "Mr. Ryan, the boy has lived with you since the accident that claimed the lives of his mother and father two months ago. During that time, you have acted in loco parentis, providing an environment of continuity and stability. Of course, it was natural and relatively easy for you to do so. Since your late sister and her husband lived next door, I understand you often undertook care of your nephew when they were alive. But that does not diminish your prompt and compassionate action in ensuring your nephew's ongoing welfare at a time of great personal loss to yourself."

Agitation ruffled over Kim, and she turned imploring eyes on Gordon Sorenson, her lawyer. Do something! she screamed silently. There was absolutely nothing natural or right about her nephew's living anywhere but with her.

Sorenson laid a hand placatingly on her arm. Easy, his glance warned her. Don't hand him victory on a plate. She knew he considered her a difficult client, given to unpredictable outbursts that had seriously prejudiced her case.

"However," Judge Wilder continued in measured tones, "the demands of your profession take you out of the home during the hours when a child under the age of two is awake and active, and during that time, he is cared for by your housekeeper and her husband, neither of whom are related to the boy."

Adam raised his eyebrows and offered the merest nod of agreement. How calm he appears, Kim marveled, knowing that her own flushed appearance was symptomatic of the turmoil she was trying to subdue. Of course, the formal proceedings of the courtroom that she found so unnerving were commonplace to him. He was a district family court judge himself, and at thirty-eight, he was one of the youngest on the circuit.

For an instant Kim wondered if she could not demand that the hearing be dismissed on the grounds of conflict of interest or collusion. Adam and the Honorable Margaret Wilder were, after all, colleagues and could conceivably be living in each other's back pockets. But even in all her distress, she knew better than to give the notion serious consideration. Adam Ryan would never stoop so low. He didn't need to. He oozed unimpeachable ethics and was, on the surface at least, certain of his suitability—his right—to Jason.

"On the other hand, Ms. Forester"—the judge's gaze swung to Kim, laser sharp and entirely unreadable—"you are in the fortunate position of being able to work out of your home and could, foreseeably, be there to care for the child most days . . ."

Optimism surged through Kim, then died swiftly as Judge Wilder finished: ". . . if you chose to be. However, by all accounts, your present life-style would hardly accommodate the demands of a young child, and I am disturbed, to say the least, at your apparent inflexibility to adjust any aspect of your living arrangements. It seems to me that it is not beyond the realm of possibility for you to relocate to the West Coast, although it would be, I admit, an inconvenience."

Was she then, Kim wondered in silent frustration, to be expected to uproot herself from all she held dear? To abandon the cosmopolitan sophistication of Boston and bury herself here on the Pacific Coast in order to qualify as a surrogate parent? Some small but vital spring tightened in her brain, jarring its ordered rhythm with a tension that had been threatening for weeks—ever since Greg had been killed. Only with difficulty was she able to maintain a facade of composure.

"The course of action you have proposed—that of taking the child to live with you in your garden apartment—would be disruptive to Jason's well-being at this time, and I frankly see little prospect of his receiving from you either the stability or the maturity he requires in a parent."

Judge Wilder's gaze softened momentarily. "I regret, Ms. Forester, the deep distress your brother's death has

11

caused you, and this court offers you its heartfelt sympathy in your loss, but it is my belief that Jason has suffered the greater deprivation."

She paused briefly and surveyed the room at large. "In the interests of his future welfare, I am awarding preferment of custody to his uncle, Adam Ryan, with the proviso that his aunt, Kimberly Forester, be granted reasonable access."

Reasonable access? From a distance of more than three thousand miles? The tension spring in Kim's mind tightened further, her vision narrowing darkly as the migraine that had threatened all day burst free. A thousand tiny hammers pounded at her temples, and she turned beseechingly to the man beside her.

"If it please the court—" Gordon Sorenson was on his feet—"I move that my client be granted equal rights, with the option to take the child to her home in Boston for six months of the year."

"Motion denied," the judge replied without hesitation. "We're talking about a human being, Mr. Sorenson, not a piece of luggage to be shipped back and forth across the country. Advise your client that she has leave to apply for new consideration when and if her circumstances change. Court dismissed."

"All rise," the bailiff intoned.

Sorenson reached down to cup Kim's elbow, urging her to her feet. "Hang on," he murmured as the trembling consumed her.

But she seemed less and less able to do that. How could she hold herself together when she'd just lost everything? The pain in her head was almost blinding her. "Get me *out* of here!" It was a plea of utter desperation, for Adam Ryan was crossing the room unhurriedly to where she stood.

"Kim?" His eyes, cool and dispassionate, swept over her, missing nothing. "I don't want to make this any harder on you than it has to be. Any time you want to come out to visit, all you have to do is call."

"Get away from me!" Her voice trembled dangerously. "I don't want you to come near me."

Sorenson, embarrassed and alarmed, placed himself between them. "She's understandably upset, Judge Ryan."

"Don't apologize for me." She stepped around her lawyer and raised haunted eyes to Adam's stony features. "Who do you think you are, offering me favors? I don't need your permission to see my nephew, and I'd rather have my teeth pulled than accept hospitality from you." Her voice was becoming shrill. Even in her distress, she sensed the distaste on her opponent's face, and she knew she was digging herself into an ever-deepening hole. It might as well have been her grave.

"I'm sorry you feel like that. Maybe you'll change your mind when you're feeling better," Adam suggested quietly.

"Don't hand me crumbs when you know I'm starving." She held out her hands beseechingly. The toddler would give focus to her life; he was her last precious link with Greg. "I'll give you everything else—the house, the land—if you'll let me have Jason."

The implicit sympathy in his gaze vanished. "We're talking about a child," he reminded her icily, "not a commodity to be traded for something of equal value."

Another minute in his company and she would shatter into a hundred bits and pieces. With glazed composure, she turned away and stilled her trembling mouth with rigid fingers. She could not bear to look at him a second longer. Without another word or a single backward glance, she walked out of the courtroom and out of her nephew's life.

Somehow she made it back home to Boston, to Muldoon, her Irish setter who loved her unconditionally and devotedly, and to Evan, the one person left on earth who really understood her. Not because he was a psychiatrist but because he'd been Greg's friend, and so he was hers.

"Oh, Evan," she cried softly, despairingly, when he came, at her request, to see her, "my life is such a mess. Greg's gone, and I've lost Jason. I have nothing, no one, except you and Muldoon. And my head . . ." She pressed her middle finger to the bridge of her nose, her finely drawn brows contracting in pain. "I have such a headache, Evan. Please help me."

Her pinched expression tore at him. Bereavement had done enough, robbing her of her effervescent sparkle; losing the child had sapped the last of her strength and her spirit. She was exhausted, running on nerves that had wound down like a tired clock.

He cradled her securely in his arms. "It will be all right," he murmured soothingly. "You haven't lost everything. You still have me and Muldoon."

The dog had been Evan's gift to her on her birthday the year before. Soft as butter and adoringly uncritical, Muldoon came to her now and placed his handsome head on her knee, sensing her distress.

"See?" Evan said. "You're not alone, Kim. We'll take care of you."

She slept on and off for nearly two weeks, with no interest in doing anything but replenishing her strength. Then, one day, she opened her beautiful eyes and, catching sight of Evan, announced: "I'm starving. What's for breakfast?"

The soft gold of her hair was tarnished and lifeless, and she was thinner than he'd ever seen her, but at the indignation in her voice, he smiled and knew the worst was over. "What would you like?"

"Eggs Benedict with real English muffins, hot coffee, and freshly squeezed orange juice. None of that frozen stuff you're so fond of," she warned as she reached up to push the hair away from her face. "Ugh, I must look a fright." Memory and pain clouded her eyes. "Time for the princess to wake up and face reality," she said somberly. "I can't sleep the rest of my life away, can I?"

Of course, it wasn't that simple. She'd recharged her body, but it was going to take more than sleep to restore her confidence.

"I'll never see Jason again," she wept several days later. "I can't face Adam Ryan, not after the way I behaved."

"Of course you can. He's not going to hold that afternoon against you. He knew how upset you were."

"Upset?" The tears stopped in their tracks. "Evan, we're talking about the man who fought me in court and won. 'Upset,' " she declared bitterly, "isn't in his vocabulary, nor is 'hysteria' or 'uncontrolled.' He doesn't suffer emotions like the rest of us. He lost his sister, and as far as I can tell, it hardly caused a ripple in his life. He's made of stone."

"All the more reason for Jason to know you, then," Evan replied, caught agonizingly between professional detachment and intense personal involvement. He had to encourage her to try her wings again, to prove to herself that she could still fly, but he knew he might lose her when she did. "After all, he's as much your nephew as Adam's."

"But Adam has custody, and I—I was deemed unfit." She stared out the window at the children playing in the park across the street from her apartment, her face mirroring a sorrow and uncertainty he would gladly have erased, had it been in his power to do so. "That judge," she reflected bitterly, "how could she go against me like that? You'd think she'd have understood how I felt."

"Do you ever think that she might have made the right decision?"

Kim sighed. "Perhaps. I guess it was obvious I couldn't have coped with a child then. Heavens, I was hardly fit to look after Muldoon—or even myself. But do you know how it makes me feel to know that another woman told me I wouldn't make a fit parent?"

It was August before she allowed herself to believe that she might not have lost Jason completely. "You know," she told Evan over dinner one night when he'd come for a visit, "I need a change of scene. I'm getting stale, marking time. I haven't touched my drawing board in months."

The restless uncertainty he'd detected for days in her tone was gone, replaced by a new sense of purpose. He glanced at her. She looked very chic tonight, very self-possessed, and quite dazzling in a linen suit the color of wild primroses. This was not the same woman who'd come begging for his help three months ago. "What do you have in mind?" he asked, half knowing what was coming and half dreading her answer.

"I'm moving west. I'm going to do what I should have done all along. I will not be shut out of Jason's life."

Evan cleared his throat. "Er . . . when did you decide this? And why?"

She shrugged elegantly. "The idea's been growing on me for some time. And what's to keep me here, after all? There's no one special in my life—I can take Muldoon and all my precious antiques and heirlooms with me." Her smile was charmingly rueful. "At least I'm not likely to lose custody of them."

Evan suppressed his unprofessional urge to protest such cavalier dismissal. She had to do this—she had to put her new-found confidence to the test—and he had to give her his blessing. "Go," he said, his breathing suddenly tight, his chest aching. "As long as you're sure this is what you want. And as long as you remember I'm always here if you need me."

She searched his carefully unemotional face as she touched a hand to his cheek. "I'll remember."

He covered her hand briefly with his. "So, how are you going to go about it?"

"With extreme common sense. I'll have all my things packed up and shipped out there, then I'll drive out with Muldoon. It'll be a sort of holiday for us, before colder weather sets in. And when we arrive . . . Well, we'll see what happens."

"Don't try to rush things," Evan urged. Her expression was impish with secrets, the old sparkle back in her eyes. On the surface at least, she seemed totally in control of her life again, yet he wished she would lean on him a little longer.

But it had been five months since her twin had been killed, three months since she'd lost the battle for custody of his son. The crisis that had made her so needful of Evan was past, and it was time for her life to move forward again.

CHAPTER TWO

Three weeks later, she and Muldoon made it. They crossed the United States from Massachusetts to western Washington, arriving late one bright September afternoon to the scene of defeat with a whole new plan of attack. Adam Ryan had won the battle, perhaps, but not the war.

Of course, he would know at once that she'd come belatedly for her nephew, and he'd watch her every move. She'd have to present a dazzlingly accomplished front whenever he was around, bob figurative curtseys, put a lock on her unruly tongue—in short, do whatever was required to persuade him that she was a changed woman from the uncontrolled hysterical creature he'd last seen.

Her brother's house was a gem, so utterly charming in fact that she had to keep reminding herself that next door was Ryan territory, and that the natives would surely be hostile once they detected her presence.

Crossing the living room in resolute strides, she opened the French doors on the west wall, stepped onto the covered veranda, and inhaled mightily. Charming it surely was, but after nearly six months of vacant tenancy the house smelled musty and airless. Leaning on the railing, she scanned the territory to which she'd fallen heir.

The view was magnificent, looking out across the water, with little humpbacked islands breaking the force of the Pacific swells running up the Sound, while to the north, a distant line of snow-capped mountains rimmed the horizon.

A soul could replenish itself here, she thought. Find a measure of peace. Maybe living on the West Coast wouldn't be such a hardship after all—even though Adam Ryan was her closest neighbor.

Her thoughts ceased their erratic wandering and fastened on the name. Ryan. Judge Adam Ryan. With such a stolid, respectable title, he might have been a Bostonian instead of a small-time lawmaker from the rain forests of Washington. He was the one in the driver's seat, and she would have to act suitably humble and impressed with his accomplishment. She must give him no further opportunity to question her attitude or her stability. She must be Little Miss Sweet Cheeks, even if it choked her.

"Muldoon!" she called, banishing the unwelcome intrusion of Adam into her thoughts. "Muldoon, come!"

He'd flashed by her the minute he was released from the car, yodeling with canine joy, his ears flapping, his tail thrashing in ecstasy. She could hear him, somewhere below the rocky promontory on which the house stood, yipping with excitement at the cheeky Pacific tides encroaching on his new territory. A dog's life indeed! Her own should be as joyfully uncomplicated.

She was glad she'd decided to bring him, though. He was her security blanket, something warm and loving to curl up against when the loneliness came and shrouded her like cold Atlantic fog. Besides, every boy should have a dog, and Muldoon was a prince, his Irish setter forebears almost as distinguished as Kim's own impeccable ancestors. Jason would adore him.

Reassured by the dog's appearance on the path leading to the veranda, she turned back to the living room. Painful though it may be, she had to inspect the rest of the house. If Greg's ghost was lurking in the corners, she might as well deal with it at the outset. Better get it over with, explore all the rooms, face any lingering memories;

19

then she could begin imprinting the place with her own personality.

It was a small house, nothing more than a main floor and a dormered attic, but it bore the stamp of the Forester taste for expensive elegance. Downstairs, there was, in addition to the living room, a tiny entrance hall, an afterthought of a dining room, and a kitchen. Upstairs, the one bedroom ran the length of the house, with an adjoining bathroom boasting, she was glad to see, modern plumbing.

But settling in was not as straightforward as she'd envisaged. The sun was well down on the horizon by the time she'd unloaded the provisions from the bug-spattered Porsche. When she went to stash her perishables in the refrigerator, she found within the withered remains of something that had presumably once been edible. Lifting it carefully with a pair of stainless steel tongs, she went to rid herself of it in the disposal unit only to discover, all its costly fittings notwithstanding, that the kitchen was not equipped with even the simplest one. And horror of horrors, there was a dead mouse in the cupboard under the sink!

The large spool bed, a legacy from Cousin Roberta Tyler, whose mother had gone down on the Titanic, was covered with Aunt Martha Forester's hand-crocheted bedspread. And there was a spider, large and hairy legged, leapfrogging across it when Kim, utterly exhausted, went to sink to her rest that night. All was not sunsets and seascapes in the wilds, she reflected wearily, her initial scream of distaste having alerted Muldoon to the presence of the intruder. The idea of playing pioneer woman was beginning to strike a distinctly sour note. How had those stalwart souls endured frontier life?

Thoroughly awake, she found her thoughts turning to Adam. She hoped he wouldn't be too formidable an adversary. There was something about that winter gray stare of his that chilled her. She had the feeling he would not easily forgive her behavior at the court hearing.

Surely, though, she still had some rights? The blood tie was equally strong on her side of the family, and she was a woman, young and healthy. She could afford to devote herself to motherhood, given a fresh chance. And she could cope with all the stresses of parenthood now. She was well again.

As for Adam, he was middle-aged by comparison, thirty-eight if he was a day, a professional too absorbed in his work to have time for a wife, let alone a child. Who'd want him, though, with that air of aloof arrogance that mantled him more thoroughly than his judicial robes? Imagine having to sleep with a man whose professional image never slipped, who probably dealt with love with the same impartiality that he pronounced sentence in court.

"A cold fish," Greg, on his one visit to the East after his marriage, had said of Adam. "Thinks sex is a chore reserved for Saturday night in a dark bedroom. Doesn't approve of me at all."

It had been a graphic description, conjuring up a forbidding Victorian image, and she had rolled with merriment in her chair at her twin's assessment of his brother-in-law.

The dim outlines of the room blurred as she remembered that last time with Greg. Not all Evan's help, not even the passing of time, could ease the pain of some memories. How could a life so vital and effervescent have been snuffed out in the flip of a car on a rain-slick highway? How could her soul mate of twenty-eight years be extinguished so that not a trace of him remained? The ache in her throat told her she had been wiser than she knew to wait before coming here. Any sooner and she could not have borne it.

21

By eight the next morning, she'd eaten breakfast and tidied up the cottage. The movers weren't due until ten, which left her time to explore the terrain, to find the nearby beach that her lawyer, when he'd handed her the keys, had assured her would bring her unadulterated pleasure.

Muldoon charged ahead of her in the early sunlight, then suddenly veered off at a tangent in pursuit of some strange new scent, leaving her to find her own way. The path, though overgrown, was easily discernible, bearing the evidence of Muldoon's recent trampling. Bordered by salal and giant fern, it ended on a smooth outcropping of rock overlooking the ocean.

Across the small sheltered bay at her feet, sprawling elegantly on its own terraced bluff, was the sort of dwelling featured in glossy, expensive magazines: a cedar and glass composition that blended perfectly with its rugged natural surroundings yet promised untold interior luxury. Most impressive! And dropping down lightly to the pale, clean sand was a lithe, tawny creature clad in swimming trunks of a brevity that left little to the imagination, a towel slung nonchalantly around his neck. It was Adam.

Blithely unconscious of his wide-eyed audience, he walked to the water's edge and waded ankle deep in the waves, his hands hooked on lean hips as he surveyed the quiet morning. Kim exhaled with care and ran a cautious tongue over her dry, parted lips, her eyes aching from the strain of her absorbed scrutiny.

It was Adam; of that she was certain. The chiseled profile, the helmet of sleek dark hair, the stance: everything was there, just as she remembered it—except for the sober, conservative clothing.

Would she ever forget her first meeting with this aloof, strangely attractive man? She'd flown from the East to identify Greg in the impersonal surroundings of some large Seattle hospital she never wanted to see again. And Adam had been there to perform the same grim service for Jocelyn.

Gordon Sorenson, Greg's lawyer and later hers, had introduced them. "Judge Ryan, this is Mr. Forester's sister from Boston. She's here . . . for the same reason . . ." His voice had trailed away in sympathetic confusion as Kim and the judge had eyed each other warily across the comfortless little room.

There had been a sudden and irrational animosity in the air as each had sized up the other, accusations of blame for their painful and separate losses swirling unspoken between them.

His face was of the kind that once seen was never forgotten, a daunting collection of aristocratic planes and angles arranged in unsmiling uniformity like the head on an ancient coin. At first, she'd thought he was from the police department, there to gather grisly details of the accident, but the title "Judge" had quickly corrected the impression. In any case, he was far too well dressed. This man looked more like a forbidding James Bond, immaculate in his dark suit. He could have rolled in mud and emerged with not a hair out of place.

A surge of horror welled up in her now as Adam turned from his contemplation of the open sea and waded lazily to her side of the bay, apparently immune to the icy sting of the spray on his limbs.

Intending to steal back the way she'd come, Kim lingered a moment too long in unwilling admiration for the clean, uncluttered lines of him. He moved, she decided with a shiver, with all the deadly grace of some fleet jungle beast.

Not so Muldoon, who, having tired of the pursuit of whatever had captured his fancy earlier, came crashing through the undergrowth with all the finesse of a demented warthog. Adam raised inquiring eyes from their concentrated study of the swirling waters at his feet, and Kim spun about, prepared to sprint for the cover of the woods.

The dew lay heavy on the smooth rock, causing the leather soles of her thonged sandals to skid out from under her. Scrambling inelegantly, she fought to retain her balance and make her getaway, and she succeeded. But one of her sandals slipped over the edge, bounced once on the huge driftwood log at the base of the cliff, and came to rest under Adam's startled gaze.

Not waiting for his reaction, she fled with the setter at her heels, mortified at having been discovered watching him. By the time the walls of the cottage came into view, it occurred to her to wonder why she'd fled the scene so precipitously. Was she afraid to see him again after her crushing defeat in court? Or could it, just possibly, have something to do with the startled admiration that had invaded her as she'd eyed the elegant lines of his near-nude body?

Taking the veranda steps two at a time, she raced up to the bedroom, tossing the surviving sandal in the hearth as she made her speedy way through the living room. She had no further use for the shoe, since she'd not the slightest intention of retrieving its mate.

She had already changed into a pair of designer slacks and a cotton knit top when he came pounding on her door. Misting herself liberally with perfume and sliding four narrow jade bands over her wrist, she descended the stairs in her best lady-of-the-manor fashion, projecting a calm she was far from feeling and quite prepared to protest her innocence of whatever charges he cared to level at her.

He waited outside on her veranda, her sandal dangling conspicuously from one of his hands. She noted peripherally that he was more fully clad, though scarcely more decently. He looked like some swarthy castaway in his ragged cutoffs and faded T-shirt. Most unjudgelike! Still, any discomfiture she might have felt at the obvious reason for his visit was eclipsed in the satisfaction of seeing the sardonic gleam of humor slide from his eyes to be replaced by a look of amazement.

"You!" The word, ejected with utter shock and suspicion, caused an unholy glee to leap through her. Perhaps he was as nervous of her as she was of him. He'd immediately sensed her reasons for coming to the West Coast. It was obvious from the guarded expression that swept over his features. Her arrival was clearly the last thing he'd expected.

"Hello, Adam." Her voice conveyed the very essence of social courtesy. It was almost sunny in fact, so great was her delight at having won round one of the long fight stretching ahead. "How nice to see you again."

"Why are you here?"

Had the man no social graces, accosting her in such a frosty tone? "Why, I'm sure you know exactly why I'm here. I want to get to know my nephew." She made her eyes round and huge in their innocence, knowing full well their effect on the male of the species, though never expecting him to respond like other men.

Surprisingly, his animosity fell away, and something suspiciously close to a smile curled at the stern mouth. "Do you?" he inquired with deceptive gentleness. The intense regard that accompanied his words was as blatant as the caress of a lover. It lingered on the separate features of her face, trailed with insulting intimacy down her throat to encompass the fullness of her breasts with such familiarity that her nipples puckered in outrage.

Apprehension skittered up her spine. He was up to something. "Indeed, I do," she retorted with unnecessary force, then strove to restore that well-bred imperturbability to her voice. "After all, he is my nephew."

"Wonderful!" He raised glowing gray eyes to her face

25

again. "Let's go over right away and I'll introduce you. His name is Jason, by the way."

"I know that," she snapped, aware that her composure was slipping badly despite her every effort to hold it in place. "Unfortunately, I can't leave the house just yet. I'm expecting the moving men any moment."

"Ah, I see." The rebuke, just detectable beneath the gentle understanding, was calculated to ruffle her. Echoes from the past flitted over her—Judge Wilder's disapproving comments: ". . . disturbed . . . at your apparent inflexibility . . ."

"Don't be unreasonable, Adam. Obviously I have to be here to let them in. I'll come over as soon as they're gone."

He raised wicked black brows and regarded her mildly. "Did I touch a nerve?" he asked kindly. "I'm so sorry. Of course there's no hurry. He's waited this long, after all."

"Take a look around, for heaven's sake. Do you see a lackey lurking in the background? If I'm not here to let them in, who'll do it for me?"

"Why do you need moving men? The place is furnished."

"I've shipped out some of my own furniture and my clothes, and I could hardly have strapped them all on the roof of a convertible."

"But why bother? I understood you were planning to rent out the place."

"Whatever gave you that idea?" Such wishful thinking!

"I got the distinct impression that you thought anything west of the Appalachians was beneath contempt. Why would you want to hang on to a shoe box like this?"

"For exactly the reason I gave you. So that I can get to know Jason. I wasn't expecting Tara complete with grand staircase and chandeliers."

Her attempt at wit didn't divert him. "Why this belated interest in the boy?"

With deadly aim, he'd pinpointed the one question she

26

feared the most. With a monumental effort at calm, she tilted her head and met his gaze. "Given my way, it would have been sooner, as you very well know. As it was . . ." She shrugged with commendable sangfroid. "I needed time to set my affairs in order." She had needed time to pull herself together and take responsibility for her own life before she tried to do the same for Jason. But that wasn't the sort of observation she was about to make to Adam.

"But you're here at last, prepared and willing to give Jason the benefit of your undiluted love and attention."

What a talent he had for reducing her actions to laughable pretensions. "Yes." She would not back down. "I can afford to devote my time to him now."

"What about your job and all the other sacrifices you'll have to make?"

"I'm self-employed, remember? Relocating is merely 'an inconvenience.' "

He ignored the sarcasm. "You're some sort of artist, as I recall. Do you make enough money to live on?" He cast a disparaging eye at her designer outfit, obviously finding her faultless attire at odds with his concept of *arty*.

"Not all artists are eccentric, or starving, you know." She flicked an imaginary speck of dust from the cuff of her blouse. "I design children's clothes, and I do it rather well. I presented my new spring line just last month, and it was very well received." Her aplomb was mushrooming in step with her blossoming confidence. It wasn't so very difficult, after all, to stand toe to toe with him.

"I'm truly impressed." He accompanied his words with a second slow reconnaissance of her body, his lips pursed slightly, as though he were checking the merchandise for flaws, amusement flickering in the depths of his gray gaze. "I believe this belongs to you?" He dangled the sandal in front of her, laughter simmering in his voice.

"I can't imagine why you'd think that," she declared

27

with all the brazen nerve she could muster, stubbornly ignoring the voice inside that warned her she'd regret her foolish denial. Yet, to admit she'd been spying on him was too embarrassing.

"You weren't at the beach this morning?" He raised his brows in feigned surprise. "I wonder who it could have been, then?"

"I'm sure I don't know. I'm new here."

Suddenly, the sober mien he'd gone to such pains to maintain cracked into a full-blown grin that was dazzling in its unexpected charm. "Nice dog you've got there," he commented, his remarkably beautiful teeth flashing in his dark face.

With a sinking feeling, she turned to identify the true object of his amusement. Muldoon, faithless ingrate that he was, sat alertly on the floor behind her, his red coat glowing in the morning sun, his silly jaws wrapped around the mate to the sandal swinging from Adam's hand.

Wearily, Kim rolled her eyes, conceding round two to her opponent. "Give it to me," she muttered as she grabbed the offending item before he could comply with her ungracious request.

Muldoon, unusually cooperative, brought the other sandal to where she stood and dropped it at her feet. Had it been possible and not entirely beneath her, she believed she'd have enjoyed ramming both shoes up Adam's handsome Roman nose.

CHAPTER THREE

The timely arrival of the movers presented her with a valid excuse to terminate the interview with Adam.

"You know where we live," he called as he headed toward the door, unable to resist a parting shot. "When it's convenient, by all means drop in and meet my family."

He loped off before she could issue a suitably stinging reply. "We live" and "my family"—how sure he was of himself, how confident of his ability to keep her on the outside looking in. It made the prospect of besting him all the more appealing.

But there were other chores to be completed first, and the placement of the furniture she'd had shipped from Boston had to be given priority. It should have been a simple enough maneuver, except that with the house already furnished, it became an exercise in confused frustration.

"No, don't put the love seat in there," she suddenly decided after having instructed the movers that it was to go in the living room. "Put it under the landing window instead."

Brawny and good-natured, they obliged, favoring her with grins and sidelong stares. Clearly, they didn't mind how often an attractive blonde changed her mind. Strange, though, how harmless their appreciation seemed, compared with Adam's scrutiny. Their glances were directed at admiring the lady; his had been a knowing appraisal of the woman, seeking to probe beyond the distractions of the flesh to the intensely private soul of her that he must never be permitted to uncover.

"I'm not very organized, am I?" She wiped a hand across the sheen of perspiration on her forehead. "I hadn't expected the place to be so crowded."

"Tell you what, ma'am," the tallest of the three offered. "Why don't we set the big things in place, then you can decide what to do with all these little bits of stuff later."

She had to smile. "These little bits of stuff" consisted of a small fortune in antiques, proof positive that some aspects of family endured. Each piece came with its own snippet of ancestral lore, and if any was to be damaged, it would be impossible to replace.

In the end, they emptied everything from the main floor onto the driveway, laid the Oriental rug she wanted in the living room, and rearranged the furniture as she directed.

When the men and their van left hours later, she was bone weary, but the place had undergone a subtle and comforting change. It was no longer just Greg's house; it was hers, too. Combining his things and hers brought a feeling of closeness with her twin that she thought had vanished forever.

The traumas of country living might not be as horrendous as she'd believed last night. The house was lovely. And even if it didn't possess all the comforts of the Ritz-Carlton, its soothing quiet seemed to reach out and embrace her—as though it knew what difficult days lay behind her and wanted to console her.

She ran a loving hand over her rosewood writing desk then, Muldoon at her heels, went through to the kitchen. From the newly stocked refrigerator, she took out the fixings for a fast and easy supper: ham and Havarti with dill, some coleslaw, a cherry tart, and the remains of a bottle of California chablis. Not gourmet fare, but in her advanced state of hunger, it was a meal fit for the gods.

"We've made progress, Muldoon," she proclaimed with satisfaction, offering him the last piece of cheese. "And this is only the beginning."

It was after one the next afternoon before she had completed all the tedious but necessary chores of settling in and could get down to the main business of the day. Slapping closed her appointment book, she made her way upstairs. It was time to change into something that would bolster her confidence and underscore her suitability as a surrogate mother with the Ryan household. Not an easy task, she discovered, wishing she owned something in ruffled gingham. Adam was clearly the type to be impressed by the Little Susie Homemaker image.

Finally she was ready to attack, all dolled up in cream silk slacks and matching blouse, gold hoops at her ears, her hair in a sensible bun but artfully softened with carefully casual little wisps curling at her temples. Adam had a tiger by the tail, whether he knew it or not.

Her confidence, so buoyant as she left her own property, was eroded by the sophistication of the Ryan residence, and she was acutely conscious of the blank expanse of glass confronting her as she followed a paved path from the beach, up the bluff, to the lower reaches of the garden. Was Adam standing at one of the huge windows, watching her progress, with that supercilious little smile plastered on his face?

The path meandered through a rose garden and ended, finally, on a flagstone terrace set with white wicker furniture. Beyond sliding glass doors, she could see into a sort of library, dim beside the brilliant outdoors.

Tentatively, she rapped on the glass. "Hello?"

A marmalade cat snoozed in the shade of a planter filled with geraniums, supremely indifferent to her arrival.

31

Irked by the nervous tremor in her voice, Kim rapped again. "Adam? Are you home?"

She was met by silence, unbroken except for the ringing sound of metal on metal, somewhere at the back of the house. Following the noise around the house, she found herself on the edge of a belt of trees, and there, not more than fifteen feet away, was Adam.

Stripped to the waist, he had his back to her and was occupied with splitting the sawed logs at his feet. Fascinated, she watched the ripple of muscle across his shoulders and down his back as, with both hands, he swung the heavy sledgehammer above his head and brought it down with a resounding crack on the metal wedge driven into the upended log before him.

The sweat on his body glistened in the sun, imparting a satin polish to the smooth amber skin. Faded jeans hugged his hips, clinging like a second skin to his straddled limbs before disappearing inside the sturdy Kodiak boots he wore.

There was a rhythm to his movements, an athletic coordination, that drew her unwilling admiration. Many more displays such as she'd been treated to in the last couple of days and she'd have to revise her original image of him. *Middle-aged* seemed suddenly inappropriate, whereas adjectives such as *earthy* and *sexy* swamped her senses. This was dangerous thinking!

She was tempted to slip away, aware that her mind was growing clouded with unseemly irrelevancies, but a shadow suddenly rose from the undergrowth and came bounding forward.

The black and cream German shepherd was calm but cautious at the sight of a stranger, and Kim froze, images of bared fangs filling her mind. The dog sniffed her feet and, with a cold persistent nose, traveled the length of her leg to where her hand hung motionless. Seeming to approve her scent, the animal thrust its nose into her palm and sat back on its haunches. Reassured that she was not in danger of being torn limb from limb, Kim bent down and patted the handsome head.

There was a sudden cessation of the background noise, and the Kodiak boots she'd noticed earlier appeared abruptly beside the dog. Kim withdrew her hand and slowly raised her eyes. Adam stood with his feet planted apart, and from her lowly perspective, his legs seemed to stretch forever, to be topped by the head of dark hair, for once dishevelled and plastered to the damp forehead.

Impaled by his gaze and unnerved by his silent reception, she flung herself into conjuring up her most assured and winning mien. He simply must not guess at her alarming reaction to his proximity. But the heat from his body was reaching out like an aura and permeating her skin, which must account for the flush that was creeping over her cheeks.

It was all too silly for words. She positively did not find sweat an aphrodisiac, and backwoodsmen held no appeal for her at all. If her heart was racing—and from the erratic leap of her pulse, it would certainly seem to be doing so—it was purely excitement at the thought of seeing Jason again. Meanwhile, she must do her best to project an aplomb she was far from feeling.

"Nice dog you have here," she commented airily, then clapped a betraying hand to her mouth. They were the very words Adam had used yesterday as he'd watched her make a complete fool of herself over the sandal.

From the smile that illuminated his eyes, she knew she'd revived the same memory for him, too. "Daisy doesn't care for shoes," he told her dryly.

Dusting off her hands, Kim rose to her feet. She was at enough of a disadvantage, without groveling before him. "I'd like to see Jason."

"Just like that?"

"If you don't mind. I set aside this afternoon especially to visit him."

"But that may not be convenient for us . . . Or doesn't that matter?"

"I didn't realize I had to make an appointment to see my own nephew. Would you have preferred that I phone ahead?"

"You were expected yesterday." There was mild reproof in his tone.

"I couldn't make it earlier," she replied defensively. "I had to hire a gardener and—" She stopped momentarily, daunted by his raised eyebrows, then continued, "Well, you saw what a mess the grounds are in. I can't imagine why you let them get so overgrown."

Pointedly ignoring her comment, he reached forward and grasped her wrist, drawing it toward him, his fingers warm and firm on her skin. At his touch, her pulse, which she'd subdued with difficulty only moments earlier, leaped into frantic rhythm again. What did he have in mind?

"Jason just might be up from his nap by now," he observed, glancing at her watch. He held her wrist a moment longer, impersonally, almost clinically. And then, shockingly, he massaged its throbbing inner surface with the ball of his thumb.

It was the briefest of contacts. And then he relinquished his hold, but it left her wildly shaken. Once again, she felt as if she'd been caressed, intimately, in a secret, forbidden place by a lover too bold and thrilling to resist.

"Nap?" Feeling more foolish by the minute, for she was not normally given to such lurid imaginings, she linked her fingers behind her back so that he wouldn't see their trembling.

"Yes," he murmured gravely. "Children his age usually take afternoon naps."

She glanced up quickly, suspicious of his mocking tone. "Well, of course they do. Everyone knows that."

"Even you." His eyes were silver gray in the sun, shaded by silky black lashes of astonishing length.

He wasn't conventionally handsome, but something about him was disturbingly attractive.

"What are you staring at?"

Confused, she dropped her scrutiny to the dog. "I was just wondering how Jason feels about the shepherd. Is he afraid of her?"

"I wouldn't keep her if he were." Unhurriedly, he strolled over to where his shirt was draped over a stack of newly split firewood.

She watched him shrug into it. He left the top buttons undone, revealing, she decided, an unnecessary expanse of bare chest.

"I'm a very responsible person," he continued, jarring her attention away from his long brown fingers casually tucking his shirttail into the waist of the low-slung jeans. There had been a slight emphasis on the first word, a thinly veiled implication that she didn't share his virtues.

"I hope you are," she returned evenly. "That's my nephew you've got there."

Something flared briefly in his eyes, an acknowledgment, perhaps, that she'd scored a point. "Mine, too," he reminded her.

He let her precede him around the house, directing her to the southeast corner where the kitchen opened onto a paved patio. It gave him a chance to regroup his wits without her observing him.

He wished she hadn't come. Why couldn't she have stayed in Boston? It was the resemblance that unsettled him, of course. She was unmistakably the other one's twin, as golden and gorgeous, as capricious and careless. What whim had brought her out here after her impassioned declaration more than four months ago that she'd never bend to his will? And how long before she left again, as suddenly as she'd arrived?

35

But she was lovely and spirited and altogether too damn alluring. Her fragrance bewitched him, made him behave like a callow youth taking his first secretive peek at a girlie magazine. He'd found himself inching close to her, just so that he could tantalize his nostrils with the scent of her—a bouquet of clean, fresh woman and something mysterious and erotic.

He was ashamed to admit that the way her body moved under her clothes tugged at his gaze when he would far rather have looked elsewhere. It annoyed him that he couldn't ignore the way her hips swung with her easy, elegant stride, that something in the proud tilt of her head struck a responsive chord in him. She was every inch the thoroughbred and she knew it. And his response to her was completely unreasonable.

He hadn't intended to touch her, sensing somehow that to do so was to flirt with danger. But once the texture of her was warm against his fingers, he'd had to savor the satin quality of her skin, testing its flawless surface like some connoisseur of female flesh. Not yet forty, and already he was turning into a randy old goat!

"This way." He gestured to the open door, congratulating himself on the even tone of his voice. He sounded thoroughly respectable, pleasantly aloof. No one had to know that inside he was churning with confused irritability, at a loss to explain why this woman could tempt him to fantasize about getting to know her very intimately. This was the shrill hysteric who'd tried to barter a piece of real estate for the child she professed to want to care for. That was not something he'd forget in a hurry.

She hesitated at the glass door leading into the kitchen and turned again to watch him. At his murmured command and emphatic hand signal, the dog dropped to the patio, her ears pricked, her eyes following his every movement.

Did he exact the same unquestioning obedience from Jason? she wondered. That would certainly fit the image she'd always had of Adam—until yesterday, that was. It annoyed her to find that on the strength of two brief encounters he wasn't at all as she wanted him to be. It confused her, too. Could Greg have been wrong—no, *mistaken*—about his brother-in-law? Could she?

All at once, Adam lifted his eyes and caught her searching scrutiny of him. They neither moved nor spoke, yet Kim knew that each had recognized the electricity of their connection. Jason was not the only common meeting ground. Something much more basic, much less tangible, was struggling to emerge between them. It showed in the frisson of excitement that whispered over her skin, in the wary depths of Adam's gaze.

He cleared his throat, crossed to where she waited, and held out his hand, palm upturned. "Please, come in." And before she could sidestep the contact, he clasped her elbow in the warm magnetism of his fingers and ushered her into the cool interior of the house.

"Damn!" The child, his chubby calves beating a tattoo against his high chair, waved his spoon delightedly at his uncle.

Kim recognized him at once, although he'd grown considerably in the last few months. Startled at the greeting, she turned to Adam.

His expression, dark and forbidding, melted into a smile of almost comical pride.

"Damn! Damn!" The oath tripped from the toddler's lips with the easy familiarity of frequent use, to Kim's appalled consternation. What sort of environment was this in which to bring up Greg's son?

"Hey, sport!" Unperturbed, Adam hoisted Jason out of the chair and swung him toward the ceiling. "How's my boy?"

"Lively, as usual."

Adam turned to where a pleasant-faced woman was preparing vegetables at an island counter. "Wearing you out, is he, Mrs. B?"

Kim was astonished at the change in Adam. Since stepping into the house, he was a different person—tolerant, affectionate, relaxed. Watching the interaction among the three—the way the woman sliced celery sticks, handed one to Jason, then, at his wounded expression, another to Adam—Kim saw what she could be up against: a tight little family circle with no place or need in it for her.

It would have been a truly discouraging realization an hour ago, before that silent acknowledgment of mutual attraction between her and Adam. But a chain was only as strong as its weakest link, and she may have found his vulnerable spot. He wasn't nearly as flinty-hearted as he'd like her to believe.

"Where's Tom?" Adam asked the woman.

"Vacuuming the pool, I think. Er . . . will it just be you and Jason for dinner, Judge?"

"Yes." He didn't look up from tucking the toddler's shirt into the top of the corduroy shorts he wore.

Kim was growing increasingly annoyed. The woman—Mrs. Bee, or whatever—was eyeing her with avid curiosity. And Adam was living down to all Kim's expectations of him—either too boorish to effect an introduction or too ignorant to know his social obligations.

"I don't believe we've met," she announced in her best Boston manner. "I'm Kim Forester, Jason's aunt."

"Yes . . . I can see that." The other woman was clearly shaken. "How do you do? I'm Claudia Baxter, the housekeeper."

"Don't undersell yourself, Mrs. B. You're a lot more than that." Adam, straddled across a chair, seemed as oblivious to the tension in the room as he was to Jason's tugging fistfuls of the fine black hair on his chest. "We couldn't do without her, could we, Jason?"

"Damn!" Jason crowed obligingly, bouncing on his sturdy little legs, his bare feet steady and trusting on Adam's denim-clad thigh.

Glory be, did no one find it unseemly that the child had the vocabulary of a truck driver?

"Would you like some iced tea or something?" Adam turned to where she still stood by the door.

"I could bring it out to the patio, Judge," the housekeeper offered.

"Thanks, Mrs. B. On the west terrace, though, so Jason can get some sun."

"I'll keep an eye on him in here if you'd like to visit with Ms. Forester alone."

"No." Kim stepped forward, tired of being treated as if she weren't really there. "I'd like to spend the time with Jason." She glanced meaningfully at Adam. "That's why I'm here, remember?"

"You bet." With an economy of movement that left her no time to anticipate his intention, he uncoiled from the chair and plunked Jason unceremoniously into her arms. "You take him and I'll bring the tray."

With a howl of outrage, Jason wriggled in her nervous grasp, squirming around to reach out again to Adam.

"Jason!" Adam bent down, his hands on his knees, his eyes level with the boy's. "Hey, don't cry."

Unhappy at being clutched to an alien bosom, Jason renewed his efforts to escape, giving noisy vent to his displeasure. He was an extremely slippery child, Kim concluded, wincing as a flailing fist struck her in the eye.

"Ouch!" At a complete loss to know how to quiet or console the boy, she endeavored to turn him around, but Jason would have none of it and arched his body rigidly. She was willing to bet he'd been oiled, just for the occasion. It was impossible to secure a firm hold of him. Practically wrestling with the furious little boy, she was dismally aware of her silk shirt rumpling under the onslaught and escaping from the waistband of her slacks —and fully conscious of Adam's interested observations of her attempts to control the child.

"Damn!" Jason wailed.

39

Predictable enough, Kim thought, struggling to maintain some sort of grip on him.

"Right here, sport. See?" Adam ran a gentle finger up the little boy's cheek and, as the noisy sobs abated slightly, continued in a soothing voice, "Don't cry, son. Look who's come to visit. Say hi to Kim."

Eyes as gray and clear as Adam's peeked out from behind balled fists, and at the sight of the strange face so close, Jason's lower lip trembled anew.

"Oh, dear!" Adam turned to Kim solicitously. "He doesn't seem to have taken to you."

She had been on the verge of conceding defeat and handing the toddler back to Adam, but the words and that hateful smirk of his alerted her to the object behind his gesture. He'd known very well that Jason wouldn't welcome being thrust into the arms of a stranger. This was just another way of pointing up her surrogate inadequacies.

"Give him time," she replied with a heroic attempt at serenity. "He'll settle down." By some miracle, she managed to turn him so that he was looking over her shoulder and able to see the familiar room. When the tense little body relaxed, she instinctively stroked his back and set up a stream of soothing chatter, cooing so winningly that Jason consented to peer again at her face.

Almost immediately, his attention was caught by the gold hoop earrings. Babbling with pleasure, he lunged for them.

"Better watch out," Adam cautioned. "He's very strong and determined—like me."

"Nothing I can't handle," came her pointed reply.

"Well, good. In that case, let's go have our tea."

Leaving her no choice but to follow him, he strode out of the kitchen and down a long hall to the library Kim had found earlier. Passing through, he waited for her on the terrace, setting their iced tea on a glass-topped table.

Jason, amazingly recovered and quite intrigued by the

40

new face and its gold hoops, was exploring Kim feature by feature, poking and patting her curiously. He was a beautiful child, ash blond as she and Greg had been when small but with Adam's luminous gray eyes haloed with long dark lashes. He was going to break hearts someday. Maybe he'd already started, she thought, at the sudden poignant ache that assaulted her.

"Why don't you sit down?" Adam broke the silence. "He's quite an armful."

"Thanks." Settling Jason on her lap, she bounced him gently and let him examine her watch.

Conversation was difficult all of a sudden. She was intensely conscious of Adam's scrutiny, knowing he was gauging her and Jason's reactions to each other. She felt as though she were on trial; one false move and she'd be sent on her way, found unfit. Thankfully, Jason had settled down some. "Does he talk much?" she asked, desperate for some topic to break the silence.

"Nonstop as a rule." Another sly dig at her presence as he set down his glass and strolled to the stone parapet bordering the terrace.

"Damn!" Catching the movement, Jason swiveled his head in mild distress.

"Right here, Jason."

Determinedly, Jason pushed away from Kim and slid down her legs to the floor, his eyes following Adam's every move with as much devotion as she'd noticed in the dog.

"What else can he say—besides that word?"

Adam propped himself on the wall, his legs outstretched, an expression of delighted amusement inching across his face. "You don't approve," he stated.

"Well, no. Do you?"

"Sure. It's my name, after all."

Pink annoyance tinged her cheeks, but it was directed at herself for having missed the obvious. *'Dam*—not

41

damn—for *Adam.* She would have thought it sweet, clever even, had she discovered it for herself.

"He's not two yet. He'll grow out of it long before kindergarten." Adam spoke to her in the same patient tone he used with Jason.

"Okay, Adam. I concede to your superior knowledge and experience where Jason's concerned, but I can live without your snide references to my lack of experience. You *should* know more about him. You've had a big head start on me."

"That was your choice."

"There *was* no choice, as I saw it then. Proximity lent a hand in your favor, but nothing alters my right to a share in his upbringing."

"I do have custody." It was a gently uttered reminder, lethal with unspoken threat. Hands off! The boy is mine.

His smooth assurance galled her, and she was greatly tempted to fling down the gauntlet and be done with pretense. She wanted equal rights—at least—and would settle for nothing less. But caution overcame impulse, and a smile lighted up her eyes at the absurd but wise adage that danced in her mind: Softee, softee, catchee monkey! Or to coin a more familiar expression, she'd catch more flies with honey than with vinegar. She was going to charm the pants off Adam Ryan—figuratively speaking, of course—and he wouldn't know what had hit him until it was too late.

"What's so funny, Kim?"

Oh, wonderful! He sounded uneasy.

"Kim!" Jason wheeled about and marched back to her, standing squarely before her on the flagstones.

"He is—adorably so. Does he only speak in monosyllables?"

"Pee-pee," Jason announced, lamentably after the fact, staring down at his feet with enormous satisfaction.

Her question answered, Kim reared up in alarm as the toddler showed every intention of clambering up and

42

hoisting his soggy bottom onto her lap. What did one do in such situations? "No, no, Jason," she declared ineffectually, holding him at arm's length.

"Up," he demanded imperiously, doubling his efforts to scale her silk-sheathed limbs.

"Very amusing, I'm sure." Indignant at Adam's soft snort of laughter, she pointed Jason in his uncle's direction. "Since you're having such a good time, I'll let you handle him."

"Too much for you already?" Treating her to another sample of that disarming grin, Adam scooped Jason under one arm like a bundle of laundry. "What happened to 'adorable'?"

She was still searching for some scintillating gem of repartee as he disappeared inside the house with his chortling burden. There seemed no point in remaining. He'd won this round, despite her having scored a point or two.

But she was only part way through the rose garden when he caught up with her. "Throwing in the towel so soon?" he inquired, laying a hand lightly at the back of her waist.

"Not in the least," she returned faintly, all her sensual awareness converging on the area of his touch. What an unearthly sensation he was creating with his casually courteous gesture. "But I did seem superfluous . . . for the moment."

He leapt to the sand and held out his hand to assist her down the last rough-hewn step in the bluff. Almost fearfully, she allowed him to grasp her arm. It would never do to let him discover his effect on her. He wielded quite enough power already.

"Thank you." She would have pulled free at once, but he seemed disposed to let his fingers linger, allowing them to trail lightly down to her wrist, then to encircle it firmly. She was captivated by the lean, dark strength of his elegant hand against her honey-kissed skin. And when, ultimately, she was able to tear her fascinated gaze away, it was to have it drawn irresistibly to the aristocratic and unsmiling face above her.

She would have spoken, probably something inane and woefully inadequate, just to preserve a semblance of normality, but the expression in his light gray eyes halted her. If they were indeed the windows to his soul, then here was a man in mortal combat with something far more formidable than a mere woman threatening his parental tenure. There was no fear, no doubt, as to his ability to overcome the obstacle, but there was scorn in their depths and grief and a cold, implacable anger. And underlying everything else, passion, hot and consuming, fighting to subdue all other emotions.

Even his voice was different, for once stripped of its quiet, lazy calm. It was harsh, matching the abruptly spoken words: "We have to establish a few ground rules if you really intend to remain here."

"I intend to stay."

"I was afraid you'd say that." He sounded resigned. "Then will you have dinner with me tomorrow night?"

"At your house, with Jason?" Maybe she'd been mistaken; maybe he did want to work things out.

His reply disabused her of any such notion. "Certainly not. This isn't a social invitation."

CHAPTER FOUR

How did one dress for dinner with a man when the occasion was not "a social invitation"? Kim found herself giving the matter her most serious attention.

Flies and honey, she chanted to herself the next afternoon, remembering her resolution of the day before. Adam might think the evening was going to be devoted to business, but she knew better. The seed of an idea had been planted yesterday and had been germinating in her fertile mind ever since. She'd never get Jason by legal recourse. Heavens, if she hadn't been stable enough before the trial, she was technically even less fit to be a mother now after her breakdown. She had, after all, walked away from her avowed wish to take care of her nephew, whereas good old Adam, ever the constant, responsible father figure, had stood firm. But there was more than one way to skin a cat.

Surveying her wardrobe, she had, she decided, three possible options. She could wear the topaz velvet suit and project an air of sophisticated but warm feminine style. Or she could do up all thirty-six crystal buttons from the waist to the throat of the ivory pleated chiffon and confound him with her demure suitability as a parent. As a last alternative, she could slide into the black silk whose neckline plunged almost to her navel and simply lean forward every time he attempted to fix her with his severe and critical gaze or opened his mouth to talk "business."

Was there really any choice, given her circumstances?

She swept the black silk from its padded hanger and placed it carefully over the foot of the bed. She'd match her cleavage against his wits any day of the week.

He lifted the front door knocker on the stroke of seven. Still upstairs, she showered the air with her favorite French perfume and let it drift down over her hair and shoulders. An extravagant gesture for an extravagant cause.

Anticipation splashed her cheeks with rose, and before opening the door, she drew in a deep breath and tried to slow her racing heart. She might be planning to woo Adam with her army of feminine attributes, but she couldn't afford to lose sight of the stakes they were really playing for. This was not a date.

His response to her appearance was gratifying—for a moment. His eyelids, lowered perhaps in annoyance at his being kept waiting on the doorstep, flew wide, fanning his lashes in astonishment.

For a brief space, each surveyed the other before she spoke. "Come in."

She hadn't intended to pitch her voice in such a husky contralto, but she, too, was taken aback. The other Adam, she noticed almost immediately, had returned, immaculately tailored in a fine black pin-striped suit, his white shirt dazzling against his dark skin. He was a dashing sight, but he conjured up something else, too. He was an unwelcome reminder of days she preferred not to recall. The casually clad neighbor had disappeared to be replaced by the formal stranger she'd met in the Seattle hospital, the unsmiling adversary who'd so thoroughly routed her before the Honorable Margaret Wilder. It made her plans to seduce him seem trite and vain and completely irrelevant.

All at once, she wanted nothing so much as to cover her indecently bared bosom. The neckline was more than daring; it was a brazen invitation and, in the face of his suddenly tightened lips, tasteless.

46

She peered up at him from under her lashes. "I'm not quite ready. Please pour yourself a drink, and I'll be down in a minute."

She waved him to where a silver tray on the sofa table held several decanters and fled back upstairs.

"Don't take too long," he called after her, his voice resonant, she was sure, with disapproval. "We have a reservation for eight, and it's a good half hour's drive."

She couldn't change her outfit, but an artfully concealed safety pin worked wonders so that when she inspected herself a second time in the mirror, the neckline was . . . acceptable. But still, she decided, too seductive. Reaching into the velvet-lined drawer of her jewelry box, she lifted out Great-grandmother Tyler's baroque pearls and hung them around her neck. They filled the golden shadow that defined the slight swell of her breasts nicely.

Her confidence restored, she descended the stairs again to face her elegant adversary.

The restaurant was not what she'd anticipated, nor, it was clear, what Adam had expected either.

"The place is under new management," he observed with some dismay after they'd been seated in a plushly upholstered corner overlooking the ocean. "All this"—he waved a hand at the tiny dance floor—"is new."

A pianist softly coaxed the keys of his instrument, backed by a guitarist and a drummer with a velvet touch. The decor was dim and luxurious, the service discreet. It was a trysting spot for lovers, a place to touch fingers and knees, to steal brief kisses in the flickering candlelight. It was not the right setting to wage guerrilla warfare.

"It's very nice," she offered primly.

"I suppose . . ."

She should have taken pleasure in his obvious surprise. It should have given her an edge, a chance to show off her best, most polished poise. But it didn't. The candle

47

flame painted the hollows of his cheeks with mystery, veiled his eyes in shadows. And the memory of his touch filled her mind and chased away the other important things. He was a disturbingly attractive presence across the table from her—masculine and compelling. She wished he had asked her out for another reason than Jason.

"What would you like to drink?"

If she were a drinking woman, she'd have ordered an olive drowning in a double Beefeater, then followed it with a second. It might have settled her nerves, which were in an uproar. "Dry vermouth over ice, please," was the best she could do.

He barely raised a finger before the waiter materialized at his elbow. After he had ordered, Adam leaned back and regarded her solemnly. "What are your intentions toward Jason?"

Well! Even men bent on business exercised a little more subtlety than that! Whatever had happened to polite small talk? The temptation to answer directly and to pursue her case in the strongest possible terms tugged at her, but she curbed the impulse. Flies and honey, she repeated silently. Flies and honey.

"I want to be a part of his life," she replied quietly, reasonably. "And I believe, if you think about it, you'll want that, too. He's lost both parents, Adam. He needs whatever family he's got left, and I'm only sorry I didn't see that sooner."

"Perhaps." Adam's response was guarded. "But he doesn't need to be pulled apart by opposing forces. I won't let you disrupt his life just because you've decided to play auntie."

Kim pleated her napkin on her lap and prayed for patience, then lifted her eyes to his. Gray challenged golden brown, defensive and possessive. "Why do you assume we'll be opposing forces?" she asked mildly. "Don't we both want what's best for Jason?"

"I'd like to think so. It's a question, though, of what we see as best. I won't have him turned into a replica of . . ." He paused while the waiter served their drinks.

Quick anger coursed through her. "A replica of what?" she demanded. "My brother Greg? Jason's father?"

When Adam didn't respond, she continued in a low, fierce tone, "Are you planning to raise him to hold his father in the same contempt you showed Greg when he was alive?"

"That's hardly my—"

The conquer-him-with-sweetness approach was thrown out the window as reckless threats spilled from her lips. "Because if you are, I'll go back to court, and this time I'll take Jason away from you. You have no right—"

"Be quiet!" He reached swiftly across the table and laid a commanding hand over her arm. "People," he went on less urgently, "are watching us. And you do me a great disservice in supposing I would openly malign your brother to his son."

His fingers loosened their grip and briefly stroked her bare skin. Against her will and all her common sense, she found herself sinking back into her chair, relaxing. "But you said—"

"If you'd let me finish, I'd have explained myself. I will not let Jason become an indulged only child. I will not let him grow up with the same careless attitude about life and values that both your brother"—at Kim's affronted gasp, he tightened his hold on her again—"your brother and my sister showed. Whether you want to see it or not, they both had a complete disregard for life. They were young and should have had everything to look forward to. Instead, they'd had it all and done it all before they were thirty. I want more than that for Jason, and I'll do whatever I have to to get it."

He paused a moment and looked over her shoulder,

49

through the elegant dining room, and into the past. Pain and anger clouded his eyes, tightened his already firm jaw. It was a look she recognized from the day before. "You probably don't want to hear this, Kim, but Greg and Jocelyn were thrill seekers, living on the edge all the time. They were involved in a previous car accident—a ridiculous risk-taking spree—not long after Jason was born. He was six months old and in the car with them. It's a miracle he wasn't injured or killed."

He lifted his glass and took a healthy swallow, then brought his gaze back to the present and her. "And it never touched them, never gave them a moment's guilt. How do you defend that?"

"I don't . . . I won't." She gripped her own glass, her fingers numb from the icy surface. "And you have no right to set yourself up as judge. What sort of man are you to betray your sister's memory like that?"

His eyes were as gray and bleak as cold November rain. "I'm a realist," he stated harshly. "They were both spoiled rotten—takers who never thought to consider the price of their carelessness or think who might have to pay for it."

How could she have found this man attractive, even for a minute? He was all the things Greg had said he was: arrogant, judgmental, disapproving. And cruel. He was doing his best to tarnish her memories of Greg, to drag her down to his own embittered level. And he'd do the same to Jason, given the chance.

He seemed to look right into her mind. "I won't let Jason grow up like that," he warned her flatly.

"I don't want to hear any more—not your opinions or your threats." She pushed back her chair, reaching for her purse. She didn't need a homily on values from this man. Nor did she need to have flung into her face yet again how completely worthless he considered her to be. He'd said enough at the trial, condemning her for what he perceived as her selfish inflexibility.

But he rose swiftly and smoothly, forestalling her exit from their secluded corner. "Good idea," he commented ambiguously and, taking her by the elbow, led her firmly to the tiny dance floor.

It was a masterly move. Presented with the choice of clutching the table and quite literally digging her narrow spiked heels into the carpet or attempting to arm wrestle herself free of him—and in either case, putting on a floor show for the other diners—she bowed to the inevitable and ungraciously allowed him to maneuver her around the floor.

But she would not enjoy the experience. She held herself ramrod stiff, her legs jerking like some agitated marionette's, and withdrew deep inside herself.

The guitarist crooned into a microphone as the lights dimmed lower, and Kim turned her mind obstinately away from the warmth of the body so close to hers, refused to savor the scent of his cologne, the texture of his fine wool suit. He was a nobody, a nothing, and she would not admit him to her thoughts. He was ruthless and determined and he trampled over anyone who got in the way of what he wanted. He was Kim's most dangerous enemy.

" . . . you . . . in my arms . . . in the moonlight . . ." the singer warbled.

"Relax," Adam advised her, leaning down so that his voice rumbled in her ear. "Enjoy."

"I will not," she retorted in a low, furious voice.

His hands stroked up her spine, his thumb daring to cross the boundary of cool black silk to warm golden flesh, to linger there, caressingly. "I can't change what's happened," he went on reasonably. "But if you think about it, you'll surely agree that Jason should be taught a different set of values."

"I do not want to talk to you." So she was being childish. So what? She could be much worse. The urge to grind her heel into his instep was strong and violent.

"And you," Adam went on conversationally, his breath vibrating in warm little eddies against her eyelashes, "you're a spoiled little rich girl who runs away from what she doesn't want to see."

Kim responded with a furious silence. She'd heard the same thing from Evan—though couched more kindly. But then, Evan was a sensitive, civilized man who had some professional knowledge to back up his opinions. "Sooner or later," he'd warned her at one stage, "you're going to have to stop running away from painful truths. They are, unfortunately, as much a part of life as everything else, and we have to learn to accept them."

"I know," she'd replied, full of injured dignity. She'd come to terms with Greg's death, after all. If that wasn't coping with reality, what was? In any event, Adam wasn't her doctor or her friend. He didn't know the first thing about her.

". . . palm trees swaying . . . beneath a tropic sky . . ." The baritone brought Hawaii, exotic and sultry, into the room.

"But the facts remain . . ." Adam's knee nudged gently, impudently, at her thighs. A hot rush of something shamefully akin to desire swept up Kim's body, flooding her cheeks with color, her eyes with knowledge. "And you'd be a fool—we'd both be fools—to pretend otherwise."

She glared at him, defying him to acknowledge her awareness of his proximity. "Do you have any idea how close I was to Greg? How dearly I loved him? Do you"— she swallowed the lump that rose suddenly in her throat —"have the remotest idea how painful it is for me to listen to you . . . itemizing his supposed shortcomings?"

Adam pulled her abruptly against the solid warmth of his body. "Do you think it's not equally painful for me? More than painful? Jocelyn was my sister, much younger than I. Don't you think I recognize my own culpability in all this?"

"What do you mean?"

"There was a time when I could have influenced her thinking, molded her. I should have done so, before it was too late."

"You're just jealous because she loved Greg more than she loved you." What a nasty crack—hitting him with such a low blow, knowing only that she was hurting and wanting him to hurt, too.

Determinedly, Adam restored the distance between them, his hold courteously aloof. "Don't project your own warped feelings onto me."

She winced at his unerring ability to break through all the surface anger to the real heart of the matter. It was true. She had felt rejected when Greg married Jocelyn. Not because he'd fallen in love. Heavens, she'd had boyfriends knocking on her door since she was seventeen.

No. What had hurt was that Greg had put the entire country between them, and that had been a bitter pill to swallow, not his marriage. Jocelyn had been pregnant, after all, and Greg had naturally done the decent thing. But to go such a distance to be honorable? Why couldn't they have lived in Boston? It was as though he'd outgrown his childhood bond with his sister and was deliberately severing the contact between them, letting the miles convey what he lacked the courage to say.

She'd believed she'd come to terms with all that and shed all the tears she had left weeks ago in Evan's consulting rooms, yet, unbidden, her eyes filled from a fresh source. Dearly though she would have loved to blink, to lower her gaze concealingly, she dared not. The tears glimmered and trembled, ready to spill at her slightest eye movement, but she would die before she'd expose her pain to Adam.

But he saw it anyway and, sighing heavily, gathered

her to him again, more gently this time. His gesture completely undid her.

He didn't fully understand the real reason for her misery; he only knew that he wanted to comfort her. She was huddled in his arms with the stifled sobs ripping her apart. She was too little, too frail, to withstand the force of such distress, and he was powerless to alleviate her pain in the one way that might possibly be effective. He couldn't take back what he'd said. Greg and Jocelyn had both played with life like irresponsible children.

And Kim? What about her? What was this obsession she had with canonizing her brother? Had she really never seen what had been apparent to everyone else? And if not, why not? Because she was the same? God, he hoped not—for Jason's sake, of course.

Yet Jason had nothing to do with the powerful conflict that was tearing at Adam now. His mind was clicking along, smoothly in gear, his words reflecting the ordered logic of his thoughts. But his body was consumed with something entirely different. A warm urgency was flickering persistently, and it was all he could do to control it. It would be easy to let his hand encircle her more boldly, to permit an inconspicuous finger to press knowingly beneath her arm at the soft side swell of her breast; it was exquisite agony to guide her steps with the subtle pressure of his thighs and hips. He was long past his urgent youth, normally well able to curb his passions for places more appropriate than a public dance floor; however, he knew himself to be in danger of a shocking revelation of arousal if he didn't end the dance at once.

Of course, he should never have started it, yet he'd had to do something to tear his fascinated gaze away from her cleavage. It had seemed a dreadful waste that a string of pearls should occupy territory he'd suddenly longed to taste. Dancing had seemed a stroke of brilliance as an alternate form of torture, but it had all gone awry and he'd had more than he could handle.

54

He waited until she seemed calmer, then bent down to whisper in her ear. Foolishly he allowed the perfumed softness of her hair to brush his mouth. It was not a wise move. Desire raged, defying the dictates of his rational mind.

"I think we should leave," he said gravely, marveling at his steady tone. By rights, his voice should have cracked with the strain that threatened his body.

Firmly, he put her from him, ignoring her little murmur of protest and the way she tried to burrow more comfortably into his shoulder like a child. Oh, Lord, he was tired of being a father figure to everyone around him. Jason was one thing, but his mother, his sister, and all the rest who professed to be mature and adult? He felt particularly ill-suited to play the role with Kim. It was becoming increasingly clear that the response she aroused in him was far from paternal.

"But we haven't eaten yet," she objected as he led her back to their table, dropped a generous number of bills beside his half-empty glass, and directed her to gather up her things.

"I'll buy you a hamburger on the way back," came his brusque, ungallant reply.

What a confusing man he was! One minute so hatefully scornful and critical of everything she held dear, the next so sweetly gentle and comforting that she felt she could stay in his arms forever.

Her emotions were in collision, wildly tangled and impossible to unravel. More than ever, she was conscious of the powerful control he held over Jason's future and frighteningly aware that her body, willful and fickle, was tuned to another level of involvement altogether. The pleasurable ache in her womb had nothing to do with her yearning to be Jason's mother, and once again the idea prodded at her mind: the way to Jason lay through Adam, not around him. And it wouldn't be such an onerous undertaking, surely, when her body sparked into lilting anticipation at his slightest touch—as long as her mind retained control, of course.

The speed with which Adam escorted her out of the supper club and into his large black sedan was openly unflattering. In Boston her dates had practically fawned over her in their eagerness to please.

She pushed the mink jacket back from where he'd flung it around her shoulders and turned sideways in her seat. The pearls glowed luminous in the shadowed hollows of her flesh.

"I'm not dressed for a drive-in dinner," she commented tartly. She might as well have been. Apart from his initial response to her appearance, he'd seemed impervious to how she was clad. She might as well have been in sackcloth.

"I know exactly how you're dressed," came his startling reply. "And I hope it gratifies you to know that I've been hard-pressed to avert my eyes from everything you're so willing to display. I hope it gives you enormous satisfaction to learn that the feel of you in my arms has been, to put it mildly, distracting."

"Oh!" She was absurdly pleased, and for all the wrong reasons. Over the course of the short evening, it had become increasingly important that he should see her as something other than Jason's aunt.

He was, above being Jason's uncle, supremely masculine and, as such, increasingly difficult to ignore. His avuncular qualities—and they were sterling, of that she had no doubt—were not, after all, the only considerations. They might just possibly take second place to his eligibility as a man.

The glance he turned on her froze the smile on her face. "I suppose," he continued coldly, "that I'm a fool to be disappointed that even in something as important as Jason's future you should resort to playing games. How far, I wonder, are you prepared to go with them?"

She stared at him, stricken. "What a cruel, insulting man you are," she gasped.

He shrugged and concentrated on his driving, the powerful headlights of the car slashing through the dark countryside. "Am I wrong?" he inquired skeptically.

Ashamed, she looked down at her hands. Well, yes, he was wrong—in a way. She'd meant to tease him, flirt with him, bewitch him a little. Soften him up, she finally admitted to herself. It was all part of her long-range scheme. But she never intended to let the situation get out of hand. She would never barter her body so casually in order to gain something else, not even something as important as Jason. "Not exactly . . . wrong . . ." she confessed, "but—"

The car was slowing to a stop miles from any sign of civilization. Oh, no! Surely he wasn't going to put his theory to the test?

"Relax." The harshness in his voice gave the lie to her fears. There was nothing seductive in his tone, nor in the forbidding angularity of his profile. He stabbed a finger toward the windshield. "See that?"

The straight road unwound before them, a dull metallic silver splashed with black where the moon flung the shadows of the trees across it. Pleasant enough but nothing spectacular. No view of the ocean, no glimmer of snow-capped mountains.

"Very interesting, I'm sure," she observed scathingly.

"Unremarkable to the point of boring," he agreed. After a pause, he added, "Perhaps that accounts for Greg's carelessness. Absolutely nothing else explains why his car should have rolled over and ended up wrapped around a tree. This is where he and Jocelyn were killed. They were probably playing games that night, too—testing life, flirting with death."

No! Her brain screamed silent rejection of his words. It simply wasn't possible that such an innocuous stretch of highway could have exacted such a price. At the very least, there should have been a vicious curve, a sheer precipice—something more than this quiet rural road with its well-marked center line and gravel shoulders.

A trembling that threatened everything she'd worked so hard to achieve began in her soul and spread until the hands clenched in her lap shook, and she had to bite down on her lip to prevent the audible rattling of her teeth.

Adam's voice came from a great distance. "Games," he said gently, sadly, "are not always as harmless as they seem. It's as well to be sure what you're getting involved in before you decide on the stakes. The odds might not be in your favor, and you might find the price too high to make the playing worthwhile."

CHAPTER FIVE

Adam drew up at her front door and she left the car wordlessly, too shaken to utter even the most meaningless formality. The car remained parked outside for long minutes after she'd closed the door and let the black silk dress fall around her ankles.

It took Muldoon to shatter the fragile control that was holding together all her frayed edges, preventing them from ripping open and spilling grief and horror at Adam's revelations, and shame for her own silly posturings, all over the room. The dog wandered by, gave her a sleepy glance, then curled up beside the discarded gown, his coat gleaming dull red next to the length of black silk.

Like blood, she thought wildly, covering her swiftly averted eyes. Like blood on midnight pavement!

Pain tore at her, and tears poured down her face. The images, avoided for so long, swam into sharp focus with the memory of that innocuous length of highway.

He had died there, broken beyond repair, his beautiful golden youth a sacrifice to his love of danger. And with the outpouring of her shocked grief came something new: fury, more bitter than her earlier rage, directed not at fate but at Greg, for his indifference to life and well-being. Not just his or Jocelyn's but Jason's, and hers. And Adam's. For even he, she recognized belatedly, was suffering still. The sadness in his voice tonight, the bleak sorrow she occasionally detected in his eyes, the pain written in the lines of his face—all sprang from the same source as her own tormented misery.

We're all victims, she realized with new insight, the spate of tears abating as suddenly as it had begun. Life in the fast lane had meant more to Greg than everything else put together.

She plucked tissues from a box by the bed and mopped her streaming face, letting the disturbing questions surface. What if Adam were right? What if her memories were playing her false, her perspectives warped to fit her own stereotyped concepts of mourning and loss?

The doubts gathered as relentlessly as water seeking a crack in the walls of a dam. She could hold them off for now, but they were there, gathering force, and she knew with strange relief that sooner or later she would have to come to terms with them. But not quite yet.

Twice, Adam killed the engine, then started it again, but her haunted eyes hovered before him, refusing to be banished in the flaring headlights.

She'd exasperated him to the point of his wanting to shake her, but he knew that to have touched her again, even in anger, would have been to let loose passions so ill-advised that he dismissed them from his conscious mind. He could not let his thoughts stray to the womanly softness of her flesh beneath his fingers. The scent of her, her childlike innocence of the hazards inherent in her games, could not be allowed to affect him. He was sure she had no more idea of the consequences of playing the siren, with her come-hither gestures, than had a child tampering with a box of matches next to a powder keg.

The whole situation was volatile with uncharted emotions he had never anticipated. It was only sensible to drive away, to return to his own turf and Jason, the one constant in his suddenly confusing life.

And yet the hand that extended to slide the transmission lever into drive strayed instead to the ignition key and, with a smooth flick, turned it once again to off. By stopping the car at the accident scene, he had intended to shock her, to strip away her practiced mannerisms, to expose something real. It had been a stark and cruel thing to do and not one he had planned, but her refusal to accept the truths he'd tried to impress on her earlier had driven him to it. Had he succeeded too well? Was it a refusal on her part to face reality—or an inability to do so? She had looked ashen as she left the car, frozen with the horror he'd inflicted on her. What if she couldn't handle his disclosures?

When she opened the door to his imperative knocking, he both blamed and cursed the instinct that had prompted him to see her once again before the evening ended. The velour robe she clutched to her chin threatened to swallow her in its folds, leaving her looking like some frail waif left alone to cope against insuperable odds. A not inaccurate assessment, he acknowledged reluctantly to himself. He was fully cognizant of his own entrenched power where Jason's custody was concerned.

The evidence of recent tears lay in Kim's reddened eyes and nose, and to his chagrin, she peered up at him as fearfully as though she expected him to hit her. Yet it was his own body that recoiled from the invisible blow as remorse and desire slammed him solidly in the solar plexus. The sexy siren he'd started the evening with had been usurped by a defenseless child, but his body didn't seem to know it.

He held out a placating hand. "Kim . . . I wanted to make sure you were all right."

"I am," she assured him in a voice as small and chastised as her eyes were huge and reproachful.

He had no business letting such temporary physical details sway him. Heaven alone knew how ineffective he would be in court should he permit himself to be so powerfully moved by emotion for every sorry soul that crossed his path. The issue here was Jason's upbringing, not Kim Forester's fragile beauty. But when she shivered and swayed slightly on her feet, he moved quickly over the threshold and wrapped a steadying arm around her waist.

"Here," he urged, "come and sit down before you fall down." He led her to a chair beside the open fireplace, then crossed to the tray of decanters on the table behind the sofa. Had it really been only a few hours since he'd helped himself to bourbon at this same spot?

"I don't want anything to drink," she informed him in the ghost of her usual tone.

"It'll help," he insisted, feeling he must make some useful attempt to restore her strength, or his hands would occupy themselves in activities that bordered on unalloyed lechery. What was she doing to his sanity?

"I'm starving."

The words so closely echoed his own different sort of hunger that his head snapped around in surprise. She sat huddled in the chair, her feet tucked under her like a disgruntled elf, and he was torn again by conflicting emotions: should he give vent to his exasperated desire with some scathing retort or laugh at her injured expression?

"I need to eat on time," she stated accusingly. "I have low blood sugar, and I can't go for long on an empty stomach."

"And you didn't get dinner." He was a thoughtless boor, no question about it. "Show me to the kitchen, and I'll try to make amends."

"No, thank you." She was the prim Bostonian again, completely in command of herself, unwinding her legs and rising to her feet in one fluid motion. "I can manage by myself."

She glided across the room to the tiny entrance hall and held open the front door. "Thank you for your concern."

Clearly, he had outstayed his welcome, something for which his mind told him he should be devoutly grateful.

62

"My pleasure," he replied with the utmost formality as he turned and covered the distance to the door in swift strides. He was a hair's breadth away from safety. "Good night."

But to hazard one last glance at her suddenly upturned face was a fatal error. He found himself trapped in the depths of her incredible topaz eyes. The pretenses, the superficialities, were stripped away. Suddenly the whole heart of the matter—the real heart of her—was laid bare before him, and what he saw was not Jason's aunt, or Greg's sister, but a woman whose naked need for comfort outweighed all rational argument.

To hell with reason, was his last coherent thought, then the world grew dark with painful hunger as he lowered his head and let his lips drift across the soft mystery of her mouth.

Her hard-won composure crumbled at his touch. The legs that had weakened at the sight of him again on her doorstep threatened to fail her completely as the kiss became a prolonged caress that pierced her with agonizing sweetness.

There was no other contact between them, yet every inch of her—the trembling limbs, the breasts she'd flaunted with such bravado earlier—was alive to his presence as vividly as if he'd branded her all over with his touch. And when his hands came up behind her and his fingers laced through the soft fall of her hair to cup her head, the flare of arousal that coursed through her robbed her of her remaining strength and she leaned into him.

That Adam could, with so little effort, lift her to such soaring heights of delirium when other men, less threatening and far more amenable, left her unmoved was a shattering discovery. He was the single most challenging and hostile element in her life, but had he suggested it, she might, she feared, have allowed him to lead her upstairs and seduce her with a thoroughness she'd permitted no other man.

But he chose not to do so, instead dragging his lips away from hers with such reluctance that she scarcely knew where the kiss ended and deprivation began. Before she knew what he was about, he'd put her gently from him and left. And even after the car had roared away down the road, she stood there, valiantly coming to terms with this newest turn of events.

How thoroughly he'd taken possession of her thoughts was borne out by the restless hours she spent trying to sleep. She'd slip into a light doze and he'd be there, floating through dreams that were half ecstasy and half nightmare. Sometimes he reached out to free her from the web of confusion in which she was ensnared. Then everything would shift, and he'd be leaving her on a stretch of empty road, and she knew that when she turned around, something frightful would be waiting to confront her.

She rose with the sun the next morning, no closer to knowing how she could cope with an adversary so thoroughly able to rout her every logical thought and leave her craving for his company. He was the enemy. He'd hated Greg, blamed him for Jocelyn's death, considered him an unfit parent. He disapproved of everything she stood for, disparaging her values, belittling her accomplishments. It was sheer madness to hang her heart on so cold and unattainable a star.

He called her at precisely eleven forty-six that morning. "Would you like to have lunch with Jason?" he inquired without preamble. No polite amenities, no references to the night before—just straight-to-the-point business, his manner conveying more clearly than words that they had nothing in common beyond the child.

"I—yes." How foolish to permit the silly tears to sting her eyes. What had she expected—avowals of undying love?

"He eats at noon. Mrs. Baxter will be expecting you."

It was ridiculous to hope that Adam would be there, too; even more senseless to be disappointed when, predictably, he wasn't. Jason was dribbling chewed carrots over the edge of his high chair into Daisy's accommodating jaws when Kim arrived, but the only other occupant of the kitchen was the inestimable Claudia Baxter.

"Um . . . good morning."

The housekeeper looked up as Kim's shadow fell across the floor. "Oh, Ms. Forester. Good morning."

The woman was polite enough, yet Kim felt like an interloper. "You were expecting me?"

"Oh, yes. The judge phoned to tell me you were coming. He's been in court all morning and won't be home until later this afternoon."

Was it her imagination, or had there been a meaningful edge to the woman's words? "As long as Jason's here, that's all that matters," Kim replied offhandedly, then strolled over to the boy.

He'd abandoned the mess of carrots as soon as he'd caught sight of her and sat regarding her warily. The breath caught in her throat at the dual onslaught of Jason's solemn gray gaze, topped by the wheat-colored curls that earmarked the Forester genes. "Hi, sweetheart. Remember Aunt Kim?"

"Daisy!" he retorted emphatically.

The dog, Kim realized, was watching her, too; so was Mrs. Baxter. A stirring of annoyance displaced the infatuation with Adam that had preoccupied her earlier. He was doing the legally correct thing in inviting her to visit Jason, but the entire situation left her feeling so awkward that she almost wished she hadn't come.

Tentatively, she reached out to stroke the back of her fingers up Jason's cheek. "Kim," she corrected him hopefully. It would bolster her confidence greatly if, the next time Adam was present, her nephew could distinguish between her and the German shepherd.

"Kim," Jason repeated agreeably, and spat the last of his carrots into her palm.

"Have a seat, Ms. Forester. Lunch is about ready."

"Won't you call me Kim?" Her attempt to ingratiate herself with the housekeeper was demeaning and a little risky, considering the woman's careful formality, but Kim needed her as an ally, she realized. She could learn a lot from the person who'd cared for Jason on a daily basis for the last several months. And she did want to learn, no matter how difficult it might be.

Mrs. Baxter looked startled. "Well . . . if that's all right with you . . ."

"I'd much prefer it," Kim assured her, surreptitiously transferring the messy contents of her hand to a paper towel.

Jason, meanwhile, continued an unintelligible conversation with the dog, apparently losing any interest in furthering an acquaintance with his new relative. At what age, Kim wondered, did a child become able to converse like a normal person?

"Let me help." Almost gratefully, she abandoned the high chair and crossed to where Mrs. Baxter was ladling homemade soup into a Beatrix Potter bowl.

"Why, thank you." The housekeeper seemed pleased if surprised by the offer, a reminder to Kim that she had a lot of unfortunate impressions to overcome. "Would you like to feed Jason?"

"Can't he feed himself?" Prompted by the child's attempts to digest the carrot, the question slipped out with lamentable abruptness.

"Not too well with soup, but I'll—"

"Of course. What am I thinking of?" She really was inept, she realized.

Jason eyed the approaching bowl with frightening enthusiasm. "Soup, Jason," Kim explained, placing the bowl on the high chair tray. "See? Hot."

Ye gods, she was talking as if they were both retarded!

Jason watched, mercifully quiet and attentive, as she spooned up a portion of the creamy liquid and blew on it carefully. "It is hot. Be careful, sweetheart," she enunciated slowly. Enough of this monosyllabic communication. The boy was a Forester, well able to understand simple sentences, given the chance.

"Hot," Jason confirmed, smiling sweetly before pursing his rosy little lips and blowing with such vigor that Kim's hand was bathed in a fine soupy spray.

"Oh, Jason, that was naughty." Mrs. Baxter rushed over with a napkin and offered it to Kim. "I'm sorry, Ms. Forester. I should have warned you. It's a favorite trick of his."

"Kim," Kim reminded her, smiling fixedly. When she had been Jason's age, she'd known better and could, she was sure, have recited a whole litany of acceptable dos and don'ts at the table. Why hadn't her nephew been taught the same?

"Hot," Jason crowed delightedly, sloshing the spoon around in the bowl and ejecting little gusts of breath with such energy that Kim could have sworn he created waves on the surface of the soup.

"Okay, Jason, give the spoon back to Aunt Kim." She reached out a hand but was met with a fiercely resistant fist clamped around the handle.

"Perhaps two spoons, Ms.—er—Kim? It's easier on everyone when he's in one of his independent moods."

In Kim's book, children under two years of age did not exercise independence. They were docile, agreeable little creatures, far enough past infancy to be interesting yet young enough to be malleable. Weren't they? Stifling a sigh, she accepted the proffered second spoon. "Thanks, Mrs. B."

It was all very discouraging. Maybe she wasn't cut out for parenting. Not everyone was, and certainly nothing about her association with Jason was exactly coming naturally.

Gathering her patience in both hands and a few drops of soup in the spoon, she again offered the latter to Jason. "Time to eat," she insisted more severely than she'd intended, then withered with shame as he opened his mouth like an obliging little bird and obediently swallowed. Between mouthfuls, he favored her with smiles of such enchanting sweetness that she promptly revised her opinions of his shortcomings, completely bowled over by his charm.

"Mrs. B, do you suppose I could spend some time with Jason this afternoon?" They needed to spend some time alone, she and her nephew, to get away from this stilted, contrived situation and the curious observation of onlookers if they were to get to know each other.

"Well, he takes a nap after lunch . . ."

"Yes, I know he does, and I wouldn't dream of disrupting his routine. But perhaps later? Just a walk around the garden?"

"I don't see why not," Mrs. Baxter conceded. "Come back about three."

The game of tag with the tide was such a success that Kim failed to notice the lowering sun and rapidly cooling temperatures. Until a frisky wave caught Jason unaware and slapped him squarely on the bottom. The shock sent him toppling into the cold, wet sand and then what a howling he set up.

Nothing she could do—and she pulled every trick in her admittedly limited repertoire—would console him. Underneath the clumps of soggy sand, he was purple with outrage. "Come, darling," she coaxed, and attempted to gather him to her amethyst cashmere-sweatered bosom.

"Bad!" he raged as his tears trekked through the grime on his face, then he pushed away from her as though she'd made a pact with Neptune himself to humiliate him.

"Let's go home, Jason." He was beginning to shiver with cold. And Kim decided she must exercise her authority and take charge as she saw fit. The afternoon had been going so well. She'd been flushed with rosy optimism at the rapport that had sprung up between her and Jason. Now, in the space of a minute, he was resisting her with all the energy he could muster.

In desperation, she seized him and tried to balance him under one arm, much as Adam had the other day. It had looked so effortless then, and it certainly seemed the ideal way to transport a child whose arms and legs were flailing with rage.

Yet something was clearly amiss. Where Adam had scooped him up into a neat, cooperative bundle, she was saddled with a squirming, multi-limbed opponent. By the time she gained the Ryan terrace, her amethyst sweater bore unmistakable battle scars, and she was gasping from the effort of shipping home her unhappy burden.

"Having fun, little mother?"

Oh, for Pete's sake! Adam *would* have to appear right on cue, impressively dignified in his dark suit and tie. "Of course," she retorted sourly. "Mud wrestling's my favorite pastime."

He let out a shout of laughter that did nothing to sweeten her disposition. Once again, he had caught her at a disadvantage and was enjoying it. What had he done for laughs before she'd shown up?

" 'Dam!" Jason screeched, and doubled his efforts to get free.

"Here's your child." Kim relinquished her hold—and the battle. Adam and Jason deserved each other. "He's wet . . ." she flung over her departing shoulder, "as usual."

"Then do something about it."

The warning undertone in his voice penetrated her frustration. She was, she recognized, in the midst of a situation that could jeopardize any future claim she might make to wanting a serious share in Jason's life. If she walked out on him now, trivial though it all may be, it would be used against her, she knew. Bad enough to have referred to him as Adam's child, disclaiming her own connection. What, after all, was a little undignified skirmish with Jason beside her overall aspirations? "Well, certainly—if you have no objections."

"None at all." He smiled, his gray eyes gleaming with amusement. She could have throttled him.

"Well . . ." She drew an exasperated breath. "Where —what would you like me to do?"

"He could use a bath," Adam offered, his pseudoconfidential tone suggesting that only a congenital idiot would have thought otherwise.

"Oh, please, Adam." She ran a hand through her disordered hair. "Have a heart. This is all new to me."

He opened his mouth, but before he could utter a word, she went on, "Don't remind me that it was my choice. I know it and I wish I'd done things differently, but I'm really trying to make up for that now."

"Are you?" He looked down at her, skepticism clear in his cool gaze. "How do I know?"

"You don't," she said dejectedly. "I guess I'll have to prove it."

Mrs. Baxter appeared on the scene and came promptly to the rescue. "Let me take him for you, Ms. Forester. I've run the water for his bath."

"I'd love to help," Kim offered. Jason was no easy task, but anything was preferable to Adam's suspicious interpretation of her every word. Didn't he trust her at all?

However, when she looked up from emptying Jason's sudsy bathwater half an hour later and found Adam propped in the doorway observing her, the warmth in his eyes melted her festering resentment. How long since he'd come through the nursery to the adjoining bathroom to watch her inexpert ministrations to the child? And why did she feel his attention had been diverted from its original intent by the sweeping thrust of her breasts against the smooth-fitting sweater as she leaned over the tub?

"You're almost as grubby as he was," he observed, amused. "Why don't you go home, relax, and put your feet up? You look worn out."

Flustered by his kindness, she nodded and dropped her eyes to Jason, angelic in pale blue sleepers, his corn silk curls for once neatly combed. "Good night, sweetheart. See you soon."

"Kiss," Jason demanded, puckering up winningly and holding his chubby arms wide.

"Oh, Jason." Swiftly, she pulled him to her and buried her face in his sweet-smelling neck. How easily he tugged at her heartstrings—and what havoc they could wreak on her emotions, he and his uncle, if they really put their minds to it.

"Loveys." Jason smacked his lips enthusiastically on her cheek and hugged her in return.

"Love you, too, darling." Then, aware that he was growing restive in her too-tight embrace, she released him and blinked furiously. He was, without a doubt, the most adorable child in the world.

"Let's go," Adam announced as Claudia Baxter reappeared to take charge of Jason. "I'll walk you to your door."

"No need." Quiveringly conscious of him from the moment he had appeared on the terrace, and still foolishly tearful from Jason's affectionate overtures, she was beset on all sides. How did one cope with such an onslaught to the emotions and still retain a shred of composure?

In Adam's presence, one didn't, she soon learned. Ignoring her lightly uttered disclaimer, he took her elbow in a firm hold and guided her to the stairs, apparently unaware of the clamorous jangling of her nerves. Couldn't he sense the reaction his touch created?

71

"It's quite dark out," he observed. "And I'm sure you didn't think to leave the porch light on when you left your house."

"I'm not at all nervous," she protested, then promptly erupted into a mildly hysterial giggle. What a completely absurd statement! She was a jittery mess—and not because of the encroaching dusk.

"Perhaps not." Smoothly, he ushered her through the library and onto the terrace. A half moon hung heavy in the western sky, silver plating a path across the water from horizon to shore. In the cool outdoors, she was acutely conscious of the vibrant warmth of the man who loomed dark and somehow menacing at her side.

Her thoughts ran uncontrollably wild. Out here, far from prying eyes, he could attack her and no one would be any the wiser. A thrill of delicious ecstasy shivered through her at the mere idea.

She was behaving like an overimaginative schoolgirl! But despite her sternest efforts to control it, her mind refused to settle on more relevant matters, dwelling instead on the memory of Adam's lips as they'd brushed over hers last night. So soft, so gentle, so . . . tender. All completely at odds with the severe, unbending image of him she'd harbored for months—years, in fact.

"Watch your step." His fingers, cool and impersonal at her wrist as she stepped down onto the sand, triggered the most alarming response in her. It was all she could do not to gasp, softly and with the utmost pleasure, at the contact. Disappointingly, he released her as suddenly as he'd taken hold and thrust his hands into his back pockets, his palms curved around his lean, taut buttocks.

How would they feel on hers? she wondered. And then she did gasp aloud at the audacity of her normally staid New England sense of propriety.

"You okay?" His eyes were silver in the moonlight, his teeth a fleeting slash of white in his dark face.

"Perfectly. The view . . ." She swallowed once, twice,

72

then tried for a less tremulous tone. "The . . . moon is breathtaking."

"It is, isn't it?" But he wasn't looking at the moon or the sky or the spectacular sea. Captivated by the picture she'd made in the bathroom—all flushed and disheveled, forgetting for the moment to be on stage—he was devouring her with his gaze, probing past her cool Bostonian exterior, trying to find again the soft, susceptible soul of her.

And she was swaying in strange hypnosis toward him, until they were bathed in each other's warmth, not quite touching, each trapped in the other's magnetism, unable, unwilling, to break free.

When did his hands slide up to clasp her lightly at the shoulders? More important, when did hers come to rest on his chest where his heart was thudding? And how could it be that their lips were close enough that their breaths united, yet never actually touched even though desire was suddenly rampant and modesty banished? The scent of him, clean, male, woodsy, merged with the perfume of her, light, womanly, and baby powder soft, to create some unique aphrodisiac that hinted of another Adam at the beginning of time when man and woman first learned what carnal love was all about.

The man in the moon peered briefly over Adam's shoulder, then swam out of view, blocked by a head of night black hair. And the lips she remembered from the night before whispered over her fluttering eyelids, skimmed the planes of her cheek and forehead, toyed with the corner of her mouth, until she feared she'd scream from the sheer pain of wanting. Oh, such exquisite agony!

Her hands, impelled by a need she only half understood, clung briefly, spasmodically, to the linen-clad breadth of his chest, then slid around his neck to hold him fast. As though she'd uttered her desire aloud, he answered her, his mouth suddenly urgent and hot on hers, and the stars that moments earlier had winked from the farthest heavens exploded around her in a thousand brilliant fragments.

In the chaos of a kiss that melted reserve and caution before it, his hands swept down her spine in fierce possession and clasped her so bindingly to him that she was alive to the imprint of his own unleashed desire. His tongue, impatient and eager, thrust past her unguarded lips, and not for a second did she even think to prevent it as it toured and dallied over the secrets of her mouth.

It was a mere glimpse of paradise and then it was over, but she knew, as the night air rasped into her starving lungs, that nothing short of a fuller knowledge of its promise would satisfy her.

"This is madness," Adam muttered thickly, his own breathing rapid and labored. "It's got to stop."

But there was no conviction in his words, none at all. Even less in his actions, for contrary to all he said, he framed her face in his hands, the unbanked passion in his eyes blazing down on her.

"You're right," she whispered, and let him claim her mouth again without a murmur of protest. Paradise beckoned once more.

Of course, it couldn't last, all the magic of the moon and the hunger of arousal between them notwithstanding. Both were far too conscious of the lights spilling into the evening from Adam's house and the proximity of the Baxters. Kim sensed how thorough Adam would resent being caught in such a situation. A man of passion he undeniably was, and she trembled at the thought of how it might feel to be the recipient of such ardor. But necking in full view of an audience? Definitely not Adam's style. Even on such short acquaintance, she knew he'd exercise much more restraint than that.

And just as well, she told herself firmly as he released her. Foresters expected to be wooed with subtlety and finesse, and she was not about to break with tradition by permitting a near stranger to seduce her in the sand.

In any case, Adam was too cautious a man to be so cavalierly involved in a romantic entanglement with a woman who'd once opposed him in a custody battle. As for herself, a little restraint was in order if she didn't want him to guess her covert intentions.

CHAPTER SIX

He was surely in the throes of moon madness or senility or some rare fever that affected the function of his brain, Adam reflected as he retraced his steps along the beach. What was he thinking of to let himself be inveigled into participating in her games? That he was being manipulated he never doubted for a minute. Wasn't it only last night that she'd paraded before him, doing her damnedest to deflect him from his course by dangling herself in front of him?

The trouble was, he thought sardonically as he stopped at the water's edge to skip stones over the rippled surface, it wasn't really his brain that was letting him down. All the time he was schooling his thoughts into precisely the most correct response—cordial without being unduly familiar—his body was flagrantly defying him, nudging aside his common sense. And that, he knew, could lead to all sorts of developments, including emotional involvement.

And Adam knew how potentially dangerous a complication that could be. It was difficult enough to be cool-headed on the issue of Jason's custody, and he was not prepared to let himself be diverted by the one woman he had most reason to distrust. The boy was like a son to him. He'd been a part of Jason's life from the time he was a newborn. It had been tough enough to have to stand by helplessly and witness Greg's cavalier approach to parenthood, too close by far to the situation in which he'd found himself when Jocelyn was a child. The young Adam, returning from college, had been appalled at the blind indulgence of parents too caught up in their own concerns to offer the sort of guidance a growing girl needed. He was not about to repeat their mistakes with Jason. Adam had something to prove to himself. He'd already failed his sister; he wouldn't let her son down the same way.

His susceptibility to Kim filled him with unease. She was the other one's twin. Even discounting the physical resemblance, there was about her a disturbing likeness to her brother that ran deeper than the leggy, golden good looks, the sleekness that only the materially advantaged seemed to be blessed with. It was her adulation for appearances, her preoccupation with the shallower aspects of life. Jason—and possibly he himself—were, Adam suspected, merely two more possessions to be acquired, to be ranged up alongside Granduncle Bertram's antimacassars or some other damn fool item.

It was one thing, though, to be on to her plan, but quite another to combat it effectively, especially when he responded to her sexually. The smart thing would be to ignore the woman and concentrate on the aunt. The question was, Could he do that?

He must, he decided. For Jason's sake. Adam the man could afford to take chances, to have a fling with the flaky lady next door. Adam the parent could not, not when Jason stood squarely in the middle, in danger of having his life disrupted and his values warped by Kim's perceptions of life. Jason came first, and Adam would withstand his attraction to Kim Forester in order to protect Jason, no matter how powerfully he was tempted to do otherwise. Emotional involvement was out of the question. It muddied an otherwise clear issue.

Three Saturdays later, Jason celebrated his second birthday. She'd had the date already marked on her calendar and had been looking forward to it ever since the day she'd driven into town for a gift. But as the weekend drew near with no word from Adam, she began to wonder if she'd be included in any family celebrations.

On Friday, he called her. "It's Jason's birthday tomorrow."

"I know," she was anxious to inform him. "Did you think I'd forget?"

"How should I know what you'll do? You've not been exactly famous for your predictability in the past."

"Things were different then." How she wished she could erase his bad impressions and explain to him how she had briefly lost sight of the things that really mattered. Each individual dealt with grief in his own way. Surely he wouldn't punish her for not being as strong as he? Perhaps not, but confession might increase his mistrust of her capabilities even further.

"You mean you're not sulking anymore. Well, that's something, I suppose."

Hateful creature! "May I spend some time with him . . . please?"

"That's why I'm calling. Come over around three tomorrow and help him blow out his candles. It won't be much of a party by your standards, perhaps, but he's only two."

"I'm sure," she replied, gritting her teeth, "it will be lovely." He never missed a chance to put her down, did he?

They were gathered in the kitchen when she arrived the next day, the birthday boy the center of Adam and the Baxters' doting attention. Jason was on the floor, absorbed with a set of brightly colored interlocking building blocks, when she came in.

"Happy birthday, Jason." She bent down to hug him.

"Birthday," he repeated clearly, then caught sight of her gaily wrapped gift. Attached to the box by a length of blue ribbon was a helium-filled balloon. "Catch," Jason squealed, and lunged for it.

"Calm down, son." Adam held him back and turned him to face her. "How about saying thank you to Kim?"

"Okay."

He'd have agreed to anything, Kim thought in amusement, as long as he could get his hands on the balloon.

"He's a little short on manners today." For the first time since she'd come into the house, Adam looked her squarely in the eye, his expression pleasantly aloof. It was the first time she'd seen him since he'd kissed her on the beach. He'd been conspicuously absent every time she'd come to see Jason. "But he does thank you."

She might have been a distant acquaintance, one he didn't much like, instead of Jason's aunt, for all the warmth in Adam's tone.

"Let me help you unwrap your present, sweetheart." Determined not to feel like an outcast, she knelt beside the boy and detached the balloon.

"Mine," Jason insisted fiercely, pushing the box away and grabbing at the ribbon.

"Jason!" Adam warned. "Behave yourself. You can play with the balloon later."

Nothing else had been gift wrapped, Kim noticed, casting a dejected eye over the items scattered around Jason. Apart from the building set, there were a sturdy truck and a stuffed Snoopy. A very Spartan collection indeed. Nothing like the elaborate birthdays she and Greg had enjoyed as children.

With some difficulty, Jason was persuaded to open her gift, demolishing the beautiful wrapping in seconds. Reaching into the box, he hauled out the expensive kite, ran a critical eye over it, then, pushing it carelessly aside, turned again to the balloon. "Catch," he insisted firmly, addressing himself to his uncle.

The response to her carefully selected gift devastated Kim. As inconspicuously as possible, she inched backward to the nearest chair, hurt and miserable. No matter how hard she tried, she didn't seem able to succeed.

"I think," Adam said, retrieving the kite and placing it out of harm's way, "that we'll keep this until you're able to appreciate it, Jason. Although"—the sweet smile he turned on Kim brought her close to tears, and she switched her gaze hurriedly to her hands—"I might try it out myself before then."

"Ms. Forester?" Claudia Baxter was at her elbow, her voice and face full of warmth and understanding. "Will you join us for tea and cake?"

Kim swallowed the lump that persisted in her throat. "I don't want to interfere—"

"Rubbish." Adam was on his feet. "You're his aunt and you deserve to suffer the ordeal of birthday cake along with the rest of us. It will be quite a performance, I can tell you." For once there was no sting in his words. "Okay, Jason, time to blow out the candles." He placed the boy in his high chair and nodded to Tom Baxter, who'd been quietly observing the events from his seat at the kitchen table.

Claudia had made a chocolate cake, and when Tom set the candles aflame, Jason was entranced. Blowing them out once didn't begin to satisfy him.

He was still a baby, Kim realized, her equilibrium restored. He had more chocolate on his face and hands than he'd consumed, and all the excitement was beginning to make him unruly.

"I'll do it," she offered when Jason indicated he wanted out of the high chair. She lifted him clear before anyone could object. "Shall I let him down or take him upstairs for a nap?"

Adam coughed lightly and turned his face away as Mrs. Baxter hurried forward with a damp cloth. "Oh, dear," she murmured, "your lovely dress . . ."

Jason was clutching and patting at Kim's pink silk jersey shift, leaving chocolate tracks everywhere he touched. And she, if she had any brains at all, should have thought to wipe him off before she picked him up. "Don't worry about that. It's washable," she assured the housekeeper.

"And so, my lad, are you," Adam declared to Jason. "Clean him up, Tom, will you, so Claudia can serve us some of that fabulous cake of hers." He turned to Kim. "Let's go somewhere quiet to recover."

He led the way to the library and opened the glass doors. "We may as well take advantage of the weather and sit outside. There won't be too many more days like this."

He was being very kind, she thought. As if she were a not-too-bright child who needed encouragement. It didn't help her confidence any to realize he may well be right. "I—"

"That—"

They spoke together, then stopped, each waiting for the other to continue.

"Go on," Adam invited. "What were you about to say?"

She shrugged. "Nothing important."

He looked at her thoughtfully, his gaze taking in the strain around her eyes, the wary tension in her hands. "That kite," he said gently, "was a lovely idea. I hope you understand that he'll have hours of pleasure from it when he's a little older."

"It wasn't a good choice. I know that now."

"It's the thought that counts, Kim. You know that, too."

Mrs. Baxter brought in a tray of tea and birthday cake and disappeared again. "You pour," Adam suggested, "and I'll pull the patio chairs into the sun."

Kim was glad he stepped outside. It gave her a chance to blink away the ridiculous tears that seemed to well up at the least provocation, making a mockery of all her bright, shiny poise.

The late September sun bathed her in warmth, the tea restored her, and the cake—the cake was ambrosia. She looked up from devouring the last crumb and found Adam watching her, his gray eyes opaque and enigmatic.

"Look at you," he murmured huskily. "You're as bad as Jason." And so delicious, his mouth watered. "Is that dress really washable?"

Confusion dotted her cheeks. "What?"

"Your dress," he repeated, and tried not to let his gaze linger where Jason had boldly allowed his grubby little paws to stray, "can it really be washed?"

"Oh." She gave a deprecating little laugh and brushed ineffectually at the chocolate stain. "Yes. It'll look like new once it's been laundered." She found his gaze most unsettling.

"A brand-new beginning," he said softly. "Something we could all use once in a while."

What was he saying, with his quiet, lazy voice and those caressing gray eyes? "Some of us more than others," she sighed regretfully.

He continued to watch her for another unnerving eternity, then stretched his arms and linked his hands behind his head, sprawling elegantly in the wicker chair. "Stop being so abject," he admonished, disarming her with his sudden smile. "I had you all neatly pigeonholed as a brat, and here you are spoiling my image of you."

Oh, she thought at the sharp little pain that attacked her heart, it would be so easy to like this man. He had such charm sometimes, such gentleness, and such absolute, immovable integrity.

He watched the shifting expressions play over her features, disturbed again at his response to her. Things could become very complicated, he decided. He'd seen another side of her today, a side that had nothing to do with her allure as a woman, although that was an aspect of her that he was finding increasingly difficult to ignore.

There was a softness to her, a vulnerability that slid past his well-defended guard and touched his heart.

What a pity he had to be so suspicious of her motives, so uncertain of her sincerity. And without his doubts, how much simpler—and more complex—their association could be. "Drink up," he said abruptly, impatient with himself. He'd set up the rules himself, weeks ago, when he'd decided she was out of bounds except as Jason's aunt. It was up to him now to abide by them. "The sun's almost gone and you'll catch a chill out here."

She was being dismissed, she realized. Whatever had provoked his pleasure in her company, it had dispersed and been replaced by his usual reserve.

September spilled into October, and it became cooler and wetter outside, the great cedars and firs dripping with moisture. There were new and broader horizons to clothes designing, Kim found, now that Jason populated her world. Watching him at play, absorbing the realities of his life, her imagination stretched to new, exciting limits. During those times that she was not actively engaged in looking after him, she filled the pages of her sketchbook, the ideas taking shape in swift, bold strokes of charcoal, and finely detailed pen and ink drawings. And she was doing something right, because not only did she sell her designs to all her old outlets, but she cornered the market locally as well. She had more than enough to keep her busy well into the new year.

Meanwhile, she flung herself into making up for the missed months of Jason's babyhood. However complicated her original motives might have been—and Evan, her psychiatrist friend, had doubts about her real reasons for wanting the child—the issue now was pure and simple: she loved her nephew. The combination of blood tie and proximity allowed for nothing less than total devotion. The idea that she might ever be anything other than closely involved in his life was unthinkable.

Adam observed her interaction with Jason without comment. He wasn't openly critical of her efforts, but she knew he was withholding judgment until she'd proved herself to him. Sometimes, he seemed quite favorably impressed by her dedication to Jason.

But when he came home early one afternoon and found she was planning to drive Jason into town for new winter boots, he lacerated her with his anger.

"Have you lost your tiny mind?" he barked, reaching over the side of her convertible and yanking Jason out of the car.

She was dumbfounded. "I was going to put the top up," she defended herself. "I'm not a complete fool."

"That's debatable," he snapped.

"Don't be rude," she replied, offended, but she might as well have saved her breath.

Strapping Jason into his safety seat in the conservative black sedan, Adam flung himself behind the wheel and left her to converse with the trees. Honestly, if it hadn't been so much against her better nature, she'd have offered him a graphic gesture of defiance in his rearview mirror.

Nevertheless, she withered under his scorn and tried to hate him for his arrogance but failed miserably. The need to have him smile on her, to show her again the tenderness hidden under his flinty exterior, was too strong. In view of Greg and Jocelyn's untimely deaths, Adam's concern for car safety was understandable and merely underscored her own lack of responsibility.

She'd never felt like this before; she'd never experienced such a wild response to a man, and it wasn't at all the way the books said it should be. Oh, perhaps for the seconds on the beach, when he'd held her and kissed her, revealed his ardor to her in the close possession of his embrace, there could have been violins and roses. But even then, while she was still spiraling slowly back to earth, he was all aloof conviviality, if there was such a thing. One minute scorching her with the heat of his desire, the next dousing her with cool, passionless pleasantries. She seemed to affect him like some forbidden fruit, too tempting to ignore but leaving such a bitter aftertaste that his appetite and curiosity were sated with just one bite.

Yet he was not completely indifferent to her. On those days when Jason alternated between adorable and obnoxious, and Kim was so frustrated and discouraged that she was ready to concede defeat, pack her pigskin suitcases, and head east in the Porsche, it was Adam who gave her fresh encouragement.

"Don't let him wear you out," he'd say. Or, "Stop trying so hard to be perfect. It's okay to lose your patience once in a while." Then, with the smile that melted every last vestige of resentment she might be feeling: "It happens to the best of us."

Disappointingly, though, he made no further overtures such as he'd initiated on the beach. There were no spoken references to that evening, ever. Yet, just when she would decide the whole incident had been some sort of lunar hallucination on her part, he would appear during one of her visits with Jason. She'd look up from some game or other and find that Adam had entered the room quietly. And even though his words, often severely rationed and distressingly neutral, might have been intended to hold her at a distance, his eyes caressed her with silver fire.

From the very beginning, it had been the messages in his eyes that had stayed with her. She remembered that first meeting in the hospital, right after the accident. He'd looked as if he might be sick if he had to shake her hand or speak to her. The best he'd been able to manage had been a nod. Later, after his victory in court, his pity and distaste had been plain to see.

And the day he'd discovered that she was his new neighbor, sexual awareness—mutual if unacknowledged —had sprung to life between them, sparked by the knowing sweep of his eyes over her body. The mere memory made her toes curl still.

And it was the eyes now. The glances he sent her, however unwillingly, were those of a lover. He could murmur "Good afternoon" in the most casual tone, but the look that accompanied the words was as intimate as a hand on her naked breast and brought the heat flaring to her cheeks.

Between him and Jason, she felt like a soft-boiled egg upended in its cup, with two spoons beating relentlessly on its shell. Didn't they know that if they kept it up, she'd spill all her frail uncertainties in an untidy heap at their feet?

What had happened to her earlier self-confidence? She'd come west believing she was strong enough to cope with whatever was waiting for her. She'd been prepared for resistance; she had almost relished the fight she knew Adam would put up to deter her. For a conniving woman, she was hopelessly inept, letting herself be swept along on such a tide of longing. Where was her hard-headed determination to best him at his own game? How had everything gotten away from her? What had happened to her well-laid plans? How could she have let herself get caught in such an old, clichéd trap as to fall in love with the man she'd intended to cast in the role of villain?

The questions hounded her, and the fear that her mask would crack and reveal her to Adam as someone too unstable to be let within hailing distance of the Ryan household terrified her. She knew only too well in what contempt Adam had held Greg's eccentricities. What would be his reaction to outright, documented neuroticism?

She thought she was destined to find out the afternoon Adam came to collect Jason and happened across a portfolio on her couch. Uninvited, he flipped back the cover and examined the sketches. In the act of zipping Jason into his jacket, she paid little attention until Adam spoke.

"What in the name of all things bright and beautiful are these?"

The derisive tone, not to mention the words, was a warning in itself, but she refused to heed it and replied blithely, "Preliminaries. I'm working on Jason's Christmas gift." She had learned to be more practical, after the debacle with the kite. Blue jeans were almost a uniform with Jason, now that the weather was colder, so she'd decided to give him his own designer denims.

Adam raised his formidable brows and impaled her with an incredulous stare. "You're joking, of course."

"Why would I waste my time doing that? I want to give him something special, something unique. It's not every little boy who gets his own designer label . . . is it, my lamb?" She dropped a kiss on Jason's nose.

"Cookie," Jason replied equably, and struggled out of her arms to march to where she kept a jar of chocolate-covered graham crackers just for him.

"It's not something this little boy's getting, either," Adam assured her.

"It is, if I choose to give it to him," she retorted rashly, and was to wonder later what drove her to invite his abuse in such a fashion.

He lifted a sheet of drawings and held it aloft as though it smelled of something unspeakably foul. "No child of mine," he informed her, "is going to walk around with an embroidered patch on his behind."

Attack was the best form of defense, she knew, and she should have come back with: "Why not? You've got one on yours." It would have been only a slight exaggeration, since *embroidery* was a mite strong to describe the discreet logo stenciled on Adam's snugly tailored jeans.

But she allowed herself to be deflected instead by his forceful reminder of who made the final decisions in Jason's life. "He's as much my nephew as he is yours, and I don't need your permission to give him a simple gift."

"Oh, for God's sake, don't you ever learn?" he shot back scathingly. "The only thing that's simple in all this is you, Kim. Do you really think a two-year-old cares about something like designer labels?"

"It's never too early to acquire good taste—" she began.

"For 'good' substitute 'expensive and pretentious,'" Adam cut in. "I swear, sometimes I think you need your head examined."

Two references inside a minute to her mental state were too much in her sensitized condition. "You're so almighty superior you make me ill," she snapped. "Enough of you and anyone would become unhinged."

"If the cap fits . . ." he snorted, slapping closed the portfolio and standing up. He loomed over her and tapped his temple meaningfully. "Crazy lady," he murmured in parting, derision curling the corners of his mouth.

The door closed behind him and Jason, and she sank to the couch, horrified and completely deflated. If he ever found out about her weeks of therapy with Evan, it would mean the end of everything. No more Jason, no more Adam.

But that, she decided indignantly, was not going to happen. Her little depression during those months when she'd doubted her own ability to overcome the double loss of Greg and Jason was in the past. She would not let Adam drive her back; nothing, ever, would defeat her quite like that again. So why did she feel so threatened?

Flinging a harried glance at the ormolu clock on the mantelpiece, she picked up the phone. Five o'clock in the evening, Pacific time, made it eight o'clock on the East Coast. Not too late to make the one call that might get her through this incipient crisis. Feverishly, she dialed, then held her breath as the phone rang across the country. Be home, Evan.

He answered on the fifth ring. "Dr. Brewster."

"Evan!" His name gusted past her lips on a wave of such pure relief that after a second's silence he burst out laughing.

"Not quite 'heaven,' though hearing from you comes in a close second. How are you, Kim?"

It was no time to stand on ceremony. "Oh . . ." she quavered, mortified at the tears that seemed to be perpetually waiting for release, "okay, I guess."

"What's wrong, Kim?"

"Things aren't turning out the way I planned."

He was the perfect antidote to her panic: a calm and reassuring, capable professional and loyal friend. "Things seldom do, love, but that's no reason to quit trying. What's got you so upset?"

"I don't know if I can explain it." But, surprisingly, with him she could. He knew her. He could accept her, weaknesses and all. "I thought I knew what I wanted. I even intended . . ."

She ran a hand down her neck as her fingers splayed to contain the hurting lump at the base of her throat. Her voice was thick with the unshed tears. "I knew I could never win custody of Jason legally, so I thought . . . through Adam . . ." It sounded so incredibly tacky that she couldn't go on.

"You thought you'd wheedle your way into the uncle's affections and go that route instead," Evan finished for her.

"Yes," she admitted. "It seemed so straightforward at first, but it's not that simple anymore. I can't stand the thought of not being with Jason, but I can't use anyone, especially not Adam, like that, either."

"The child means a lot to you." It was more a statement than a question.

"More than I ever expected. He's real now, not just an

extension of Greg. I don't want to lose him." She paused. "I don't want to lose Adam," she added, the reality of what had been in her heart for days leaving her stunned. The huntress had been caught in her own trap!

There was a moment's silence on the line except for the hum of long distance. "There's more to your relationship with Ryan than Jason's custody, then? Is that such a bad thing?"

A bitter, pain-filled laugh escaped her. "You might say so. Sometimes he looks at me as if maybe there's some spark of feeling there, then it gets submerged in a sort of disgust—with himself and me. I guess I'm just not your basic West Coast mother type. He'd prefer me to be staid and sober and . . . old-maidish. And no matter how hard I try, I can't fit the mold."

His reply was so long in coming that she thought they'd been disconnected. "Evan? Are you still there?"

There was concern and a hint of anger in his voice when he answered her. "For everyone's sake, please don't try. If he really does have feelings for you, you can bet it's not for a sober old maid. And I'm sure that's not what he wants for Jason, either. In any case, you can't make yourself over to suit him. You're not a chameleon."

"No," she replied forlornly. "I'm a boiled egg."

Evan laughed a short, surprised bark. "A what?"

"Oh, nothing. I guess I've changed since coming here. It's funny, but the things I used to set such store by don't seem worth much anymore. I'm even beginning to see Greg in a more realistic light."

Evan's surprise came across three thousand miles in a single astonished syllable. "Oh?"

She hesitated only fractionally. "I guess I've grown up a bit. I see things now that I couldn't see—didn't want to see—before."

"Perhaps that's why you feel so unsettled."

"Perhaps. But there's more to it. At bottom, I'm really scared as to how Adam would react if"—her voice grew furtive—"he found out about my . . . case history. I'm afraid that on top of everything else it would be the last straw."

"That's ridiculous," Evan stated flatly. "For a start, you have no real 'case history.' Having difficulty coping with death is scarcely an indication of mental instability. And I can't believe a man in Adam's position can afford to be as unenlightened as you seem to fear. This isn't the nine-teenth century, you know. You've got no reason to be ashamed, just because you needed a little help getting your life back on track."

"It's just one more fault in my already imperfect char-acter. As a family the Foresters haven't exactly impressed him."

"No one's perfect," he pointed out. "And if Ryan can't appreciate you as you are, with all your warts, he's not worth breaking your heart over. Listen, Kim, if you can see the weaknesses in Greg's character without falling apart, you've come a long way. Don't fall into a new trap with Ryan."

"I don't know what you mean."

"Don't waste your energy gazing at him worshipfully. He's not indispensable, any more than Greg was."

"I never believed he was," she objected.

"Sure you did. Greg was your other half, to the point that you believed you couldn't be whole without him. Don't make the same mistake again. And be sure Adam is what you really want before you pledge your all to making him happy."

"It's how he feels about me that's the problem."

"Remember what you said when you breezed out of my office a few months ago? You were going to take things 'one day at a time.' Don't push, Kim. Things will work out."

"Oh, I hope you're right. I want so much, and I've no right to expect—"

"You have every right. If Adam can't see that, he's the one with the problem."

Somehow, Evan had managed to put his finger on the sore spot and make it feel better. "I love you," she told him. "I don't know what I'd ever do without you."

"Yeah." He cleared his throat. "I love you, too. Keep in touch, okay?"

Only after she'd hung up did the full impact of her revelations and what Evan had said hit her. Gazing worshipfully? Was that what she'd been doing? No wonder Adam was finding her so entirely resistible. The night they'd gone to dinner, he'd been far less able to ignore her.

She vowed that she would never stoop to flaunting herself quite like that again, but it was time to abandon the pitiful role, too. It didn't really suit her. There had to be another way to make Adam see her through fresh, unbiased eyes. And she'd find it, because over and above everything else, one thing was shiningly clear: she wanted the package deal—Jason and Adam—and she was going to go for it.

CHAPTER SEVEN

The following week was unseasonably mild and sunny, and when she crossed the beach one day on her way to visit Jason, she found him burrowing in the sand with a small blue pail. Adam was with him, the sleeves of his red flannel shirt rolled up to his elbows.

"I had to play hooky," he explained at her questioning glance. "It's the perfect day to build the last sand castle of the season. Come and help."

"I don't know if there's much I can do," she replied doubtfully. It was a magnificently elaborate creation with battlements and turrets enough to house an army.

"Sure there is. The place could use a woman's touch, don't you think?" His eyes lingered for a moment on hers, unreadable but not without warmth. "Stick these clam shells on for windows and stuff and make trees and things for the courtyard while I go find us a flag and something to snack on."

"Oh," she complained humorously, dropping to her knees beside Jason. "All you really want are slaves. You get to go hunting and we stay behind to do all the work."

"That's the way it should be," he retorted, squinting at her in the sun, his lashes casting dark crescents of shadow on his lean cheeks. "You know what they say: A woman's place . . ."

"Is in . . . the home," she faltered, and found her gaze imprisoned in his, undercurrents of tension swirling between them suddenly.

93

"Well," he said quietly, "for some women, perhaps."

But not for her. He might as well have said the words out loud. "For most women," she insisted, "given the right reasons."

He rose to his feet. "Ah, well," he replied obliquely, dusting the sand off his knees. "That's where the problem lies. Keep an eye on Jason, okay? I won't be long."

It always came back to that, she reflected painfully. He absolutely refused to trust her motives.

"Loveys," Jason offered, observing her out of eyes dark with anxiety and patting her cheek with a sandy paw.

"Oh, sweetie." She hugged him fiercely. "If only your uncle felt like that."

When he returned, Adam brought paper flags. "And carrot cake for us," he announced with the pride of a returning warrior.

His tone and the way he looked at her, his eyes as full of concern as Jason's had been moments before, warmed her. She knew he regretted his earlier remark. "About time," she said, unreasonably cheered. "We've earned it."

"Some job you've done, too," he teased. "Who sat on my tower?"

"That was a tower? Good grief, you could have fooled me."

"No treats for you, my lowly slave, until you learn a little respect."

"I'm truly sorry," she quipped. "Now let me have my cake."

"Uh-uh!" He raised the paper plate out of her reach. "Not so fast. It'll take more than that."

"Be nice," Jason ordered unexpectedly, and the astonished laughter that shook Adam resulted in one piece of cake falling to the sand.

"That," Kim warned, pouncing on the remaining slices and dividing them between herself and Jason, "is yours." She sat down with the child, leaned back against a log, and wriggling to a more comfortable position, proceeded to demolish the cake.

"Greedy pair," Adam complained good-naturedly. "I'm in the company of a pair of piggies."

She licked her fingers. "You guessed," she replied. "Is there any more where that came from?"

Quite a change, he thought, taking note of her blue jeans and loose sweater. She still looked delectable, but she seemed more in touch with reality of late. There was probably a designer label on her behind, he acknowledged ruefully, and he'd have been disappointed if there weren't, but at least she'd learned to leave the cashmere imports at home when she was visiting Jason. Were there other changes, too, not so easily detected?

"What are you thinking?" he asked, perching on the log, slightly behind her.

"Oh," she sighed, resting her gaze fondly on Jason, who was stuffing cake into his mouth with one hand and shoveling sand into his pail with the other, "he reminds me so much of Greg sometimes."

"Really?" Adam's tone was guarded. "I don't see it, myself."

She winced. "Because you don't want to, Adam, but he's as much a part of Greg as he is of Jocelyn."

"True," he conceded. "But I'll consider it a marked failure on my part if he grows up like either one."

When she didn't respond, he inched forward and looked searchingly at the golden crown of her head, tempted suddenly to smooth the strands of hair tossed loose by the breeze. "Kim," he murmured gently, "I'm not trying to upset you. It's just the way I feel."

She turned so that all he could see were the delicate curve of her cheek and the sweep of her lashes etched against the pale sand. "How can I help but be upset? When you diminish him, you diminish me."

"No." He grasped her shoulder with one hand. "That's not true."

"Of course it is. Don't you see? We were twins; he was my alter ego."

"But not," Adam insisted, "identical twins—biologically or otherwise. Oh, there's a surface likeness that set me back the first few times we met, but you're your own person, not someone walking in Greg's shadow. You're selling yourself short to believe otherwise."

"Don't encourage me to be any more disloyal than I already am." She closed her eyes briefly. "I know that the night you took me to dinner a lot of what you said about Greg was true, but don't expect me to thank you for it. I loved him."

Adam moved from the log and squatted in front of her, taking her chin firmly in his hand. "Hey," he said, forcing her to meet his gaze, "don't you think I know that? I loved Jocelyn, too, but that doesn't blind me to her faults. No one's perfect, Kim, but it doesn't mean they're not worthy of love."

It might have been Evan talking, except that when he'd touched her, there hadn't been this electric warmth that melted the misery and uncertainty in her heart. "No one?" she asked Adam. "Not even you?"

"Least of all me," he told her, releasing her and sprawling beside her in the sand. "It's all very fine for me to dispense advice to you, but you were only a child yourself when Greg was growing up. There wasn't much you could have done to change him. I don't have that excuse with Jocelyn."

"Do you need one? You weren't her father."

"No, but I was a good bit older than she. I saw things happening with her that really disturbed me, and I did nothing to stop them. Because of that, I've always felt sort of responsible for the way she turned out—so wild and all."

"Sometimes," Kim interjected reflectively, "when a person feels abandoned, she does wild and crazy things to cover up the hurt, and the less she succeeds, the wilder she becomes."

He angled a searching glance at her lovely profile. "Does she?" he asked quietly. "When did you become so wise?"

"Not soon enough. I thought that by getting myself caught up in a mad social whirl I could deny Greg's death. But I had to face it, sooner or later, and by the time I did, I'd done such a lot of damage and made things even worse than they already were."

"It hasn't been easy for you, has it?"

She shrugged and changed the subject, nervous about what she might disclose if they continued along the same lines. "Tell me more about your parents. Was Jocelyn young when they died?" She knew nothing of his background, she realized. Somehow, the idea of anyone as self-sufficient as Adam having parents seemed incongruous.

"Hell, no! They're alive and well and living it up in the Bahamas."

"Jason has grandparents?" She was astounded. "Does he ever see them?"

"Rarely," came the terse reply. "There's not much room in their lives for a grandson. They're too busy playing golf and impressing all the right people at all the right clubs."

"They don't know what they're missing."

His eyes went winter cold. "Sure they do. Why do you think they stay as far away from him as possible? They can't be bothered with him, any more than they could with Jocelyn. When my father made his fortune in lumber, everything else took second place to wealth and what it could buy."

He rose abruptly to his feet. "It's time I got Jason inside. It's growing cool out here. Do you want to come with us?"

"Not today," she replied softly, and stayed where he

left her, watching the sun slide lower into the sea, her thoughts as inevitable as the tide, which even now was edging up the beach, lapping at the walls of the castle and eroding its foundations. By morning, there'd be no trace of it remaining, just a stretch of sand washed clean and waiting for the new day's impressions.

Like her life, she thought in some wonder. In bringing her such comfort and enlightenment, Adam had given her a freedom to face the future that she'd never thought to hold again. Even her most private secret—her break-down—seemed less menacing since his revelations of his failings. If he truly didn't look for perfection in her, why should she expect it of herself? Unreasonable or not, she felt a surge of hope that her dreams might one day come true.

In the middle of October, Rosemary Halley, who lived with her husband a few yards down the road, sent out invitations to her annual salmon barbecue, and Adam was disturbed, to put it mildly. Not to accept would be unthinkable. The occasion was a tradition among the residents of the peninsula. But this year Kim would be invited, too, and he feared his good resolutions to keep her at a distance would take another beating by an evening of purely social contact.

His life, once predictable and neatly compartmentalized, was in a shambles. After thirty-eight years, of which at least half had been devoted to professional advancement, material security, and decent citizenship, he was ill inclined to have his days and nights disrupted by the woman he'd vowed he could not have.

He knew what he liked, and he liked his bourbon straight, his shirts custom-made, and his women cool and intellectual, unless they were in bed. He absolutely did not need the complications—or the temptations—Kim was flinging his way.

But there she was, underfoot every time he turned

98

around, ingratiating herself—with considerable success, he noted irritably—with every member of his household. And by night, when he was entitled to a little peace, she trespassed into his dreams in situations too racy to withstand the sane light of day. He was possessed by her, and he would not allow it.

The realization, when he sauntered down to the Halleys' beach, that Kim was not there with the rest of his neighbors provoked a most unreasonable jolt of disappointment in him. Annoyed that all his fine resolutions were threatening to crumble so soon, he plunged into the party atmosphere with the desperation of a man leaping from a burning building.

These were his friends, people he could call on in an emergency. Rational, responsible, reliable people, with their feet firmly planted on the solid earth of the Pacific Northwest. He could trust them.

With a mental shake, he snapped the cap off a beer and approached the group of people nearest him. Their conviviality embraced him like a balm, smoothing away the frayed edges of his irritation. And he thought, foolishly, that he'd banished his demons, for this evening at least.

It was no more than fifteen minutes later that he felt the hair lift at the back of his neck. Turning abruptly, he raised his eyes from the bottle in his hand and met Kim's gaze as she stood poised to descend the wooden stairs that led directly from the Halley property to the beach.

They might as well have been alone, so little did the rest of the crowd impinge on his awareness of her. The hum of voices, the slap of breaking waves, and the spit and crackle of the fire all receded into the background, outdistanced by his suddenly hammering heart.

With the photographic accuracy of a high-speed camera, his mind registered the challenging tilt of her head atop her elegant neck, the golden glints of her hair in the firelight. If he'd been affronted by her blatant display of flesh in the revealing black dress the night he'd taken her to dinner, he found himself now shockingly frustrated by the concealing folds of the bulky sweater she wore. The black silk had invited; this creation tormented, merely hinting at the warm curves and hollows it enveloped. He wanted nothing so much as to bury his fingers in its softness and discover the substance of her, delineate each fragile bone, caress each pliant curve.

Chemistry flashed between them—a chemistry that would not defuse, a pull that was more than sex and all of sex. And a wild, persistent song of the heart. Belatedly, he remembered his intention to remain distant. Retiring behind the safety of social convention, he raised his drink to her, nodded affably, then turned back to the group near him.

Carefully, unobtrusively, Kim unpeeled her fingers, white knuckled, from their grip on the railing. The raging hunger triggered by his knowing appraisal had unnerved her, but she'd beat a retreat rather than let him see the extent of her response to him.

He was gorgeous. Rangy and handsome in his thick Aran sweater and cream corduroy pants, he was more man than any woman had a right to hope for. His skin gleamed amber in the firelight, his dark, level brows and helmet of black hair in stark contrast to the clothes he wore with such casual elegance.

"Kim!" Rosemary came halfway up the steps to greet her. "Come on down and meet the gang."

Forcibly jerking her rapt stare from Adam's back, Kim let her glance spill over the faces upturned to hers. Shy anxiety speared through her, for they were inspecting her with the same avid speculation Claudia Baxter had once displayed. She cringed inside her sweater and fought the temptation to back up the steps and bolt home.

What had these people heard about her?

The tempo of conversation resumed after that one pregnant lull, but the curiosity, Kim realized, had merely been harnessed behind a spate of social amenities. It hummed through the atmosphere like a high-tension wire. And nothing, it seemed, could halt the covert glances that swung from her to Adam, assessing, judging, and . . . what? Finding her wanting in some vital aspect?

She felt the disapproval of these people who were Adam's friends but not yet hers. She was "that woman from Boston." The one who thought she deserved custody of Jason. The one—tee hee!—who had designs on Adam Ryan, eligible bachelor. It was all the assembled guests could do, she thought in an agony of embarrassment, not to snicker politely into their drinks.

"How do you like the West Coast?" The conversational gambit, boringly conventional, dropped from mouths that smiled while eyes that didn't appraised her clothes, her hair, her face.

"I love it." She could feel her lips, taut to the point of cracking, stretched over her teeth in a grimace that she hoped would pass for a smile.

"You plan to stay long?" Another familiar question but one whose answer, she suspected, aroused rather more interest than her first.

"Indefinitely. This is my home now, and my family is here." Stick that in your ear, she thought defiantly at the sudden hush that greeted her words as she bared her teeth again in a facsimile of a smile.

"You mean Jason?" one intrepid soul at last ventured to ask. "Adam's boy?"

"His nephew," she retorted coolly, "and mine, too."

"Yes . . . well . . ."

They began to drift away. She had committed a social faux pas. One did not, it seemed, challenge Adam's rights, especially not when one was an outsider.

She found herself in a pool of solitude as the party picked up tempo around her. She was clearly de trop. Even Adam, whom she'd thought was at least beginning to like her, was avoiding her. Had she imagined that moment of recognition near the steps?

Discouraged, she wandered away from the group. She wasn't very good, she decided, at accepting rejection or defeat, but perhaps she should give up gracefully on Adam now, before she made an utter fool of herself.

Tense and undecided, her thoughts were so filled with Adam and his bewildering effect on her that she didn't hear his approach and almost leapt out of her skin when his hand touched her shoulder.

"Not hungry?" he inquired in the lazy voice that so well belied his acutely observant nature.

"Good grief, Adam!"

He raised his brows in mild inquiry at her alarm. "What did I do?"

"You scared me half to death, that's what." Her heart had jumped into her throat and was galloping like a runaway horse, though fear, she knew, was not the reason.

"I didn't mean to."

She pressed a hand to her throat and covered the pounding pulse, feeling strangely weak. Frenzied thoughts clamored for attention. Where had he sprung from? The last time she'd seen him, he was squatting by the fire, laughing at one of Roger Halley's fishing stories. And now he was standing so close behind her in the night that to the rest of the party there might have been only one figure under the trees.

He touched her arm comfortingly. "Do you feel like an outsider?"

Honestly, sometimes his perceptions floored her. "Does it show?"

He smiled and draped a casual arm over her shoulder. "The peninsula crowd can seem pretty overwhelming to a stranger. They've known each other so long that they've forgotten what it feels like to be new to the neighborhood."

"I don't really belong here, though. They're as suspicious of me as you are."

"Suspicious?" The word emerged husky with strange emotion. "Is that how you think I see you?"

Hesitantly, she turned her head and glanced up at his dark profile. If she could just see his eyes, read their expression. But his face was in shadow and the silence between them was throbbing with unspoken longings.

"No moon tonight." His voice, dangerously close to her ear, engulfed her in memories of the last time they'd stood together like this on the beach. If he should touch her now . . .

"No stars, either," she murmured shakily.

"Who needs them?" he whispered, and lifting her hair, brushed his lips across the nape of her neck.

Electrified, she held her breath, savoring the pleasure that shafted through her. She hadn't mistaken the moment earlier. It was happening again, that sudden glimpse of paradise. Just when she'd been ready to forfeit her dreams, he'd relinquished his awesome control and revealed himself as a man, no different in his needs or desires from any other.

"Do you suppose," he asked, sliding his arms around her waist and drawing her back until she rested against the firm, masculine contours of him, "that anyone will miss us if we leave?"

"What will all your friends say?"

"My friends don't dictate where I go, or with whom." His tongue defined the delicate curve of her ear and came to rest in its sheltered hollow.

"But they might . . . not approve . . ." The words, foolish and quite irrelevant to the moment, floated away into the night as arrows of rapture darted through her.

"Perhaps not." The velvet tip of his tongue probed the dark warmth of her ear, retreated, and surged back again, possessive and insistent. "That, however, has nothing to do with us."

Her lashes swept down to cover the naked need in her eyes, but she could no more disguise the exquisite tightening of her flesh as his hands burrowed beneath the soft angora than she could ignore the rush of passion that betrayed him.

His lips strayed over her skin, past the loose cowled sweater and down the scented silken bow of her neck to her shoulder.

"Adam . . ." She stirred in his arms, wanting to feel the texture of him, to hold him to her with the same intensity that he held her. She needed to tempt him as he was tempting her; she needed, she realized hazily, to see the desire in his eyes, to know that he was not rejecting her, whatever his friends might do.

Languidly, deliberately, she revolved in his arms. First her hip and then her breasts grazed across his solid strength in a gesture of seduction and surrender. She heard his intake of breath, then saw his features etched with hunger before they swam out of focus as his mouth swept down on hers in an explosion of passion.

No mere whisper of lips, this; no fleeting caress but a volatile assault that ignited a hunger between them that would not be easily assuaged. He pinned her to him with a familiarity that no amount of warm, sensible clothing could hide, his hold, his lips, his tongue, telling her quite plainly that this was but a prelude to total intimacy.

Except . . . they were on the beach again, and there were people within plain sight. Good grief, she thought, reeling slightly as she came up for air and saw a couple headed their way, did he do this deliberately to drive her mad with desire, knowing he was safe from any truly compromising developments?

"Let's leave," she begged him shamelessly. "Please take me home where we can be alone."

But the imminent arrival of company had restored Adam to chilling awareness of who and where he was. Certainly, he cleared his throat once or twice, covertly tugged on his sweater so that it fitted concealingly around his lean hips, even ran a distracted hand through his hair. But thwarted passion, hunger, desire? Not a trace was visible. His face was impassive, his words as far removed from romance as apple blossoms in November. "The Tatlers are headed our way," he informed her evenly.

"Would you care to invite them along?" she inquired, her own voice ragged with frustration. He had effectively soured all the magic of the moment. "There's safety in numbers, after all."

He shot her a quelling glance, stuffed his hands into the pockets of his cords, and turned to the approaching couple with what she perceived as ill-disguised relief. Saved again! was written all over him.

She was enraged, as much by the trembling that lingered in her limbs as by his enviable control. He may have the body of a god and the urges of a prize bull, but he surely compensated for both by the computerized mechanism lodged where other men kept their hearts. Ye gods, he wasn't human!

"There *are* two of you over here. We weren't sure," George Tatler wheezed jovially. "Just wanted to let you know everyone's going up to the house for coffee. In case you hadn't realized, it's starting to rain, and we'll all be a lot warmer and drier inside."

And safer! They were hovering around Adam like a pair of anxious beagles with a prize pup, Kim thought resentfully. Well, they could have him. Nodding mutely to the beaming couple, she swung by Adam, ignoring his feeble attempts to detain her, and made for the steps.

As a party, the whole evening had been a bust. She should have obeyed her first instincts and left as soon as she arrived. As for Adam, he could stay and let his friends close ranks protectively around him so that the Boston Plague couldn't touch him.

The heavens opened before she was even halfway down the road, and by the time she let herself inside the cottage, her hair hung in pitiful rattails on her soggy angora sweater. But Muldoon was glad to see her, leaping around in flattering delight at her early return, and for that, she allowed him to stretch out beside her when she finally climbed into bed. Never mind Aunt Martha Forester's hand-crocheted bedspread. Tonight she needed love, not heirlooms.

"Darling, good, loyal 'Doonie," she crooned, mollified at the way the setter rolled over and offered her unobstructed access to his ribs, groaning his ecstasy at such a display of affection. Adam could learn a thing or two from her dog.

She'd only just begun to believe in herself again, and the suspicion that Adam felt somehow demeaned by his association with her was galling, not to mention insulting. She was a Forester. He should be grateful she spared him a second thought. He had his nerve, dropping her like that the second anyone came into view.

CHAPTER EIGHT

At first, she thought it was the rain beating down on the roof that had disturbed her half dreams of Adam, and she snuggled deeper under the covers, prepared to sink back into sleep, when the sound again penetrated her drowsy mind. Her eyes suddenly wide in the dark, she sat up, the quilt clutched to her. That was not rain she heard. Something was moving around outside, and it wasn't her imagination. Muldoon had heard it, too, and, his ears flattened to his skull, was slinking under the bed.

"Get up here, you miserable coward!" she hissed, all the time straining to hear if the intruder was inside or out. Perhaps it was the raccoons on her porch. They'd upended her garbage cans more than once. But then the sound came again, and it was directly below her. Someone was knocking on her veranda doors.

Climbing out of bed, she hitched up her chaste white lawn nightgown and made her way downstairs, flicking on lamps as she went.

Adam stood outside the French doors, his hair plastered across his forehead. "Let me in," he shouted above the wind.

She opened one door a crack. "What for?" she demanded. "It might be dangerous. We're all alone."

He pushed past her. "For God's sake, woman, I'm soaked and half frozen. The least you can do is invite me in."

"You're dripping all over my Oriental rug," she informed him indignantly.

"Heaven help me! Go get a towel or something, before I make matters worse."

She dashed to the kitchen and unearthed a kitchen towel. "Here," she offered ungraciously. "Make do with this, then explain just what you think you're doing here."

He emerged from under the folds of the towel, his hair in total disarray and curling slightly. "About what happened on the beach—" he began.

"Please don't bother to explain or make excuses. Your actions told me quite plainly enough how you felt." She drew in a breath of pure humiliation.

He reached out and, grasping her by both arms, shook her lightly. "You don't have the first idea what I felt."

They were standing toe to toe, indignation simmering between them. Until his eyes drifted down to where her bosom was heaving under the soft folds of lawn and rested there, apparently fascinated by her trembling agitation. Until, mortifyingly, her body betrayed her badly and defiance gave way to an awareness that caused her breasts to bud with arousal.

"Nor you, I," she flared. "When you put your mind to it, Adam, you can be really hurtful. Did you know that?"

He lifted his eyes to meet hers. Gray clashed with flaming gold, but where there should have been ice, there was sudden fire. In the space of a second, the world tilted and all the measured, guarded responses, all the preconceived and ill-conceived notions, merged with the shadows. For now, it was just Adam and Kim, man and woman, and an instinct as ancient and tested as time itself.

His grip, once punishing and relentless, relaxed. "Hurtful?" he echoed bleakly. "I don't want to hurt you —never that." His fingers slid down to cajole the soft skin of her inner wrist until the will to fight him left.

"Then, Adam"—she drifted toward him—"why did you come here?"

His reply trembled against her mouth. "For this," he murmured, and let his lips taste briefly the soft sweetness of hers. "I believe we have . . . unfinished business . . . to resolve."

He punctuated his words with kisses that sealed her eyes shut and left her swimming in a sea of such utter pleasure that she forgot she was angry with him. When his mouth fused once again with hers, she melted before him, surrendering to his brandy-kissed tongue as it found hers and engaged it in a fierce, ecstatic duel of discovery.

Her nightgown, voluminous and virginal, swirled between them. Slowly, he tugged free the ribbon at her throat, parted the ruffled Belgian lace of the yoke, and let his fingers settle lightly on the silken warmth of her shoulder. "I have dreamed of this," he whispered hoarsely, "for weeks."

The lamplight flickered, dimmed, then settled again to a soft, even glow. Forsaking the crushed velvet of her mouth, his lips trailed along the soft angle of her exposed collar bone, then slid with potent magic to savor the sweet swell of her breasts.

She hung trapped in a trembling web of desire. "Oh . . ." she breathed, her heart racing with the wild lash of the wind-driven rain against the windows, her body acquiescing to the demands of his mouth, "oh, me, too."

He was murmuring incoherent love sounds against her breast, nuzzling the perfumed valley, seeking the rose pink crests, the unremitting strength of his thigh between hers a hot and urgent promise of a greater, more shimmering rapture to come. And she, half fainting from the pleasure of his seduction and still dazed from his sudden capitulation, sank down and cradled his head to her, neither concern for her precious rug nor her previous outrage able to compete with the frenzied, pulsating pleasure of the moment.

The wind, hurling itself with fresh fury against the house, seemed bent on saving her virtue. At the onslaught the lamplight flickered again, then abruptly died, plunging the two of them into a darkness so complete it was an almost palpable barrier between them. She felt her skin suddenly chill and damp as Adam withdrew his lips, and she wanted to cry out in despair.

Take me, she wanted to beg. Take me here—now—please . . . and never mind the Oriental rug.

But his hands lay still on her body, cruelly impersonal, and she sensed his head raised in inquiry. Ye gods, she thought in hazy disbelief. If his neighbors weren't running interference for him, Mother Nature was. And he was going to embrace deliverance and rush to restore light and safety to the velvet intimacy of the dark, she just knew it.

But he swore instead, succinctly and with such heartfelt fervor that a giggle displaced her misery. "Why, Adam," she laughed, "your clay feet are showing. Wherever did you learn such language?"

"Hush your noise," he snapped, grasping her wrists above her head as he sank his mouth unerringly to hers in a brief, punishing kiss. "Where do you keep your candles?"

"On the table behind the sofa. I'll get them."

"No." He rolled away from her and rose to his feet. "Stay where you are. I'll get them."

He stumbled over a piece of furniture and swore softly again. A match flared, and his shadow reached the ceiling as he turned toward her, holding aloft the brass candelabra. The mellow light burnished his skin to tawny bronze and washed her exposed flesh with gold. His eyes were hooded, shadowed, but she felt his gaze sweep over her, and suddenly, all her repressed fears came rushing back. Would it be right this time? Would she find with this man the magic that had eluded her with every other? Or was she chasing an impossible dream?

Uncertainty filled her, and strangely shy, she tried to restore modesty to the disorder of her nightgown.

She wanted him to fling caution out the window, to be so utterly consumed with desire that he would take her fear away. But he wouldn't do that. He would, she suspected unwillingly, be civilized above all else. She would have to call into action all the panache of which she was capable and hope it would disguise her deep-seated inhibitions and woeful lack of sexual experience.

He'd recognized weeks ago that he wanted her, but the sight of her, with her painted toes primly peeping out from under her ridiculously Victorian nightdress and her hair tumbling in disarray over her half-bared breast, gave new meaning to the word *desire*.

A usually contained and disciplined man who prided himself on his finesse as a lover, Adam experienced a sudden and shocking urge to reach out with one hand and tear the fine fabric away from her body. It seemed a magnificently appropriate way to give vent to his pent-up passion.

Instead, he lowered the candelabra to the floor and dropped to his knees in front of her. The candlelight danced and flickered over her skin. "Where were we . . ." he murmured, and kissed her deeply, "before we were so rudely interrupted?"

She disengaged her lips and lowered her eyes, a small, secret smile hovering at the corners of her mouth. "I think you were going to seduce me," she replied demurely, and walked her fingers boldly up his chest until they feathered over the fine line of his jaw.

"The hell you say." His voice very nearly caught in his throat at the blinding hunger that gripped him. His mouth swooped down again on hers as he swept her to him. He thrust the candelabra into her hands and, swinging her into his arms, rose to his feet and carried her across the living room and up the stairs.

Rain streamed down the windows, drummed on the sloping roof above their heads. The candles cast a dim, fitful glow that left the corners of the room shrouded in darkness, and the world narrowed to the high mahogany bed with its white lacy cover and goose feather quilt, its fine linen sheets and deep, soft pillows.

With care and tenderness, he lowered her to the bed and let his lips brush her face, feature by delicate feature. He was filled with the scent of her, French perfume and rain-kissed hair blending with the sweet, old-fashioned smell of lavender laundered sheets.

Pressing her down to the mattress, he framed her face in both hands and laced his fingers through her hair. Leaning his forehead on hers, he willed his body to patience. But his control was sorely threatened by her soft, willing mouth flowering under his and by the eager, questing fingers gliding over his ribs to where his heart hammered in his chest.

Still, he would have lingered, let his tongue trace a moist, leisurely path from her lips to her breasts, knowing that the night stretched before them and tomorrow was a lifetime away. But she was warm and vital beneath him; her delicate, womanly curves accommodating the sinewy contours of his body in such invitation that desire crashed down on him, shattering his restraint.

His lips never leaving hers, he drew her up to lean against him and sought the remaining ties of her gown. As the last one fell free, he abandoned her mouth and, gathering the fine fabric in his hands, eased the garment over her head. She sank back to the pillows, golden and slender and unbelievably lovely in her unashamed nakedness. For a brief moment, she lay alone as he shrugged free of his own clothing, tossing it carelessly aside and displaying to her wondering gaze the lean, athletic beauty she had secretly admired weeks earlier.

Intent on prolonging her pleasure, he leaned down and brushed his mouth lightly across the contoured angle of her cheek, rested fleetingly at the throbbing beat of her throat, then renewed acquaintance with lips that parted eagerly to the exploration of his darting tongue. He would have feasted on every inch of her, reveling in the texture and taste of her, but her hands, stealing over the taut planes of his belly, drove him to a towering urgency.

"Kim . . ." he pleaded through clenched teeth, his brow furrowed with agony and beaded with sweat, "wait . . ." But the craving was driving him to madness, and with a last despairing groan, he sank into the hot, pulsing pleasure of possession, crushing her to him in violent, annihilating passion.

She stroked his hair, brimming with tenderness for his exhausted vulnerability. He was so dear, so completely lovable, she could have held him through eternity. But no sooner had his breathing slowed to some semblance of normality than he raised his head and impaled her with a mortified look.

"Don't tell me," he said abjectly. "I'm an animal, I know."

"What?" Suspicion stilled her hands and drove a cold wedge of fear into her heart. Was he dreadfully disappointed? "What do you mean? It was wonderful."

"For me, perhaps, but"—he stopped just long enough to shift to his side and prop himself up on one elbow—"what about you?"

"Yes," she assured him brazenly, "for me, too."

He stared at her, astounded. She couldn't possibly be so naive as to believe he didn't realize that he'd sated himself on an innocent, too swept up in his own greed to recognize a virgin until it was too late. Shock carved his features into a grimace of distaste that softened as he saw her faltering expression. "No," he contradicted her softly, and reached out a finger to turn her face toward him. "Look at me, Kim."

"What's the matter?" she demanded more shrilly than she intended. "Are you saying you're sorry we made love?"

113

"Don't play games, Kim. We both know you didn't get much pleasure out of it."

She closed her eyes against his penetrating gaze. "Oh, good heavens, not that again. Honestly, you men make such a big deal about it that it makes a woman wish all those helpful sex manuals had never been written." Good grief, didn't he know what he'd given her was enough? That he'd filled her needs and given her the reassurance she'd been seeking? "The world doesn't have to stop spinning for a woman to enjoy lovemaking, you know."

"You're cheating yourself," he admonished gently, "again."

"No, I'm not. You're just worried that it makes you less of a man if I'm not groaning and writhing all over the place, and I wish we could change the subject, because all you're doing is making me feel less of a woman."

A startled laugh escaped him. "You're all the woman I can handle."

"And you're man enough for me." She sat up, at once the perfect hostess. "So, having settled that, would you care for some coffee?" Enough of all this analysis.

"Coffee?" he asked with strained incredulity. "*Coffee?*" Reaching out, he captured her with his free arm and, turning on his back, brought her head to his chest.

She could feel the laughter rumbling through him and tried to push him away, bracing her hands against his shoulders. "Stop it!" she wailed. "You're spoiling everything."

But he ignored her and brought her face down to his. She could see the candle flames mirrored in his dilated pupils; she could feel the fine hair of his chest rasping across the softness of her breasts.

"Hold your foolish tongue," he ordered huskily, and pinned her to him with indolent little kisses that rippled over her mouth and along her jaw with a strange and thrilling potency. "And let me show you what you missed the first time."

114

Smoothly, he turned and aligned himself with her, and with the utmost patience and dedication, he set about releasing her from her shy inhibitions.

It was rather terrifying. The whispering discovery of his hands over her skin lulled her alarmingly, permitting a distant rhapsody to echo through her blood. When he lifted his head to gaze down at her, a whimper escaped her, and quite against her will, her body arched up in unconcealed hunger. Something wild and free inside was struggling to escape, to shed the chains that had confined it so effectively for so long.

Shock widened her eyes. She tried to fight him; she struggled to retain control over her body. What did he want of her? She couldn't let him strip her of all her pride, all her defenses; she'd never survive if he did. But reason failed her and a slow, intoxicating elation flowed like lava through her veins as he let his mouth follow the contours of her body, his tongue trailing with dizzying impact over her abdomen to her thighs.

"*No* . . ." she gasped. But it was not his trespassing fingers she tried to deny. It was the sensations, alien to anything she'd known before, that ruffled the edges of her nerves and led her to the brink of discovery.

"Let go," he urged her, his voice deep and hypnotic. "Let me love you . . ."

And how could she not, when his mouth was suffusing her with golden pleasure, weaving impossible, irresistible magic at the forbidden, secret heart of her?

"No . . ." she begged again, faintly, but her willful body ignored her, rivulets of desire darting the length of her to join the tide of passion.

"Yes," he insisted, and brought his lips back to ravish hers with drugging kisses that paralyzed her mind and spun her thoughts into a thousand crystal rainbows that shimmered at the core of her.

She held him to her in aching ecstasy, gasping at the tremors fluttering like tiny wings in her womb. The wonderful, warm weight of his body, his harnessed strength and gentle urgency, leveled the last of her resistance, and conscious thought evaporated in the heat of her own desire.

"Kim . . ." he murmured as he sank into her welcoming warmth, laying siege to the ingenuous woman buried under the polished lady. He stripped away the layers of conditioned response, luring her until she hung trembling on the brink of ecstasy.

He would not let her escape him this time. Only when she was so enmeshed in passion, clasping him with abandon and burying her face in his neck with inarticulate, frenzied pleas, did he permit the inexorable tide to overcome him. Passion soared between them and crashed down to release a fountain of pure, sparkling rapture in Kim that plumed and cascaded along every nerve until her body was drenched with the joy of it.

Oh, she'd been right! The world did not stop its spinning. It whirled instead, so furiously that she'd been flung into some other galaxy, speeding to a new destination so glorious that she came back to earth newly born, finally and fully a woman.

She pressed her lips to the smooth skin of his shoulder, tears of gratitude oozing from beneath her closed eyelids. He'd never know the extent of his gift to her.

Turning his head, he nuzzled her gently and was horrified to taste the salty trickle inching down her cheek. "Kim?"

"It's nothing," she whispered, feeling like a fool. She reached up and touched the tips of her fingers lightly to his lips. "You're the first man to make love to me. Did you know that?"

Her skin gleamed in the candle glow, pearly with moisture. With very little encouragement, he thought dryly, he could be persuaded to repeat the entire experience. For reasons that defied logic, she had a powerful effect on his libido. She was an intoxication in his blood that no amount of cool reason was able to dispel.

Propping two pillows behind him, he ran a teasing finger down her nose. "I found out," he said ruefully, "though you might have warned me. Now explain what all that was about, earlier—all that nonsense about sex manuals and women not needing—"

"Ful . . . fill . . . ment," she finished for him, stretching out the word and arching her body like a cat's before snuggling back against him. What a lovely, smooth, sensuous word it was!

"Otherwise known as 'writhing around and groaning,' " he amended, laughter simmering in his voice.

She flushed, a lovely, translucent rose that caressed the tops of her breasts and seeped into her cheeks. "Oh . . ." Her eyelids fluttered closed for a second. "Well . . ."

"Well, what?"

"Nothing."

"Nothing? You call what just happened 'nothing'? I'm crushed."

"It was very . . . nice," she conceded forlornly. Why was he laughing?

"But not proper," he suggested with unseemly levity. "Great-grandmommy Beatrice Maude would have been shocked, right?"

She drew away from him, mantling herself in hauteur. "Probably."

He let out a hoot of mirth at her offended glare. "You're beautiful when you're uppity!"

"Don't be ungallant," she snapped. "It's just not done to discuss it as though it were an experiment."

" 'It'?" He tilted her chin up and let his finger slip down the curve of her throat until it found the dusky warmth between her breasts. "What's this 'it' you're talking about?"

She averted her face, increasingly annoyed at his persistence. Wasn't it about now that he was supposed to clasp her to him and spill forth endearments like so many priceless gems? Say the all-important "I adore you, Kimberly, my darling, my angel, my own true love"? "You're embarrassing me, Adam."

"Aha." He let his finger outline the curve of her breast, then cupped its fullness in his hand. "Did you know you're looking this way because you're embarrassed?" he asked, addressing the taut pink bud at its center.

She tried to swipe his hand away, but he caught her wrist and held her fingers to his thudding heart. "And I'm sleepy," he told her, his eyes pools of pure wickedness. "Can't you tell?"

"Stop gloating, Adam. You've made your point."

"Hmm . . . two, as a matter of fact," he drawled, and lowering his mouth to her other breast, took its eager peak between his lips.

But she wrenched away from him, her emotions wildly confused. There was a dangerous other side to being so liberated in love. It left one remarkably defenseless and open to hurt. Look at his attitude toward her already, as though she were a toy created for his not-very-subtle amusement. "That's enough," she announced. Clamping down severely on her rampant response to his touch, she swung her legs over the side of the bed. She would not be a source of entertainment for any man.

He eyed her warily. "You're upset."

"You could say so," she returned frostily.

"Let me be sure I understand the problem," he said, his tone far from serious. "You're annoyed with me because you enjoyed making love with me."

"Actually, it's your overblown ego that's annoying me. I'm about to gag on it."

"Actually"—he mimicked her Boston accent with commendable accuracy—"it's having to face reality that's got you all choked up. I should've been a nice guy and let you think you had me fooled."

118

"You couldn't be a nice guy if your life depended on it," she shot back nastily.

He felt his jaw sag slightly. Was this the same woman who'd tugged at his heart out there on the beach? What had happened to the languorous woman whose limbs had twined with his only moments earlier and made his resolutions to keep her at a distance seem a ridiculous penance only a monk would have honored?

He looked so utterly taken aback that she had to fight a debilitating urge to reach out and comfort him. But he recovered with dismaying ease, his earlier bantering tone quite faded when next he spoke. "In that case . . ."

He flung back the covers and was out of bed with an economy of movement that left her still struggling to turn her nightgown right side out. "Well," she temporized, stealthily reaching for the robe she'd left at the foot of the bed, "don't feel you have to rush off on my account." The robe had slipped to the floor, and at some point, Muldoon had stolen into the room and was curled up on it, sound asleep, impervious to her efforts to dislodge him.

"Why not?" Adam inquired sardonically. "I seem to have served my purpose."

That hurt, particularly since he was badly misconstruing her behavior. She was sorely at odds with her dearly held beliefs as to what constituted proper conduct. This . . . this *pagan* passion she'd experienced had a cruel backlash. Hot on the heels of the marvelous elation, inhibition was rushing back, more tenacious than ever. It seemed indecent, to say the least, to indulge in such luxuriant ecstasy with a man who'd uttered not a single endearment to her all night long. She felt emotionally stripped.

And physically. At that moment, power was restored, and in the sudden bloom of lamplight, Adam's cool appraisal made her woefully conscious of her unclothed bottom as she bent over and gave a final desperate tug on

119

the hem of her robe. Why couldn't he have the delicacy to look elsewhere?

Muldoon came awake with a guilty start and, seemingly anxious to atone for whatever sin he'd committed, shoved his cold nose at his mistress exuberantly. Choking back a startled squeal, she ineffectually attempted to fend off the dog; and hearing Adam's soft snicker, she shot him a killing glare. Oh, the indignity of it all!

Adam raised his shoulders simultaneously with his eyebrows, his whole demeanor one of barely contained enjoyment. "Seems there's no pleasing you at all," he drawled.

With as much speed as pride would permit, she wrapped herself in the robe's concealing folds. "You," she informed him icily, "are no gentleman."

In easy strides, he crossed to where she was haughtily drawn up to her full five feet seven inches. "What a pity," he replied, unrepentant, towering over her effortlessly, "since you're such a hell of a lady."

His parting kiss caught her entirely by surprise. Long and ungentle, it left her alarmingly weak-kneed, the taste of him lingering on her lips long after the downstairs door had slammed behind him.

CHAPTER NINE

The evening had been a ghastly mistake, Kim decided the next morning. All the lovely euphoria had seeped away to be replaced by a shattering combination of disillusionment and pain. She should never have forgotten herself so far as to permit a man like Adam to weasel his way into her affections. He was arrogant and self-serving, and for her to harbor hopes of winning his heart was pure masochism.

If only he hadn't treated her with such unfeigned amusement, she could have borne it. But the knowledge that for him she'd relinquished every last vestige of reserve, exposed the private tender core of herself, and been laughed at, albeit not unkindly, was a devastating blow.

The weather continued foul. Heavily overcast with sudden squalls of cold rain rapping angrily at the windows, it seemed as thoroughly out of sorts as Kim herself. Settled in a corner of the couch, her feet tucked under her, she glowered at the sketch pad on her lap. Disgusted, she tore off the top sheet of paper and, crumpling it in a ball, tossed it atop the dead ashes in the fireplace. How could she create innovative designs for children's clothing with Adam's laughter echoing in her mind? Widow's weeds for her lost virginity would be more appropriate!

Love had invariably been a disappointment to her, she reflected bitterly. The preliminaries—the dinners, the flowers, the tender glances—created such impossibly romantic expectations. Until Adam, she'd enjoyed the game, surrendering, up to a point. To go beyond it, she had rationalized, was to give in to an undignified lack of control. She'd always professed it to be a matter of choice, that she preferred to withhold herself, when in fact her unawakened sexuality was a closely guarded secret. From everything she'd read, she'd estimated herself to be one of the last of a dying breed: cool and untouched to the point of frigid. Until Adam, there'd never been any man sufficiently compelling to make her regret her inhibitions.

Until Adam. They were the key words. Her whole perspective had shifted since meeting him. Subliminally, she hadn't wanted to give herself to anyone but the right man. And having found him, and having given, she'd received something less than the awesome gratitude and homage she'd always envisioned.

Her head drooped forward and came to rest in her hands as a sudden wave of misery washed down her cheeks. He'd robbed her of everything with his clever, insistent hands and beguiling, trespassing lips; he'd lured her with his tenderness and virility, then gone his merry way. Hadn't she been taught from the cradle that a man was after only one thing, and that if a woman didn't snare him in marriage first, she'd be left with nothing? They had known a thing or two, those New England ancestors of hers. What a pity she hadn't chosen to heed them.

"Oh, hell!" she wailed, clasping a concerned Muldoon around the neck. The simple truth was that Adam had captured her heart, and if she'd fancied herself in love with him before last night, then heaven help her now. Because the dismal fact remained that he'd said nothing —not a single, solitary word—that could be construed as a declaration of love for her. No words of commitment, and a parting kiss that was more punishing than tender, as her bruised lips could attest. And yet she remained obsessed by him, bereft of the wit or the backbone to banish him. If this was love, she could do without it.

It was past time she took control of her own life, she decided, the unpalatable reality blundering past the barriers she tried to erect and crowding to the forefront of her mind. She simply had to stop depending on other people for her happiness and well-being. First Greg—dear, lovable, irresponsible Greg. Then Evan. And now Adam. Some people, and she suspected she was one of them, set themselves up to be victims. Well, no more.

"Idle hands," her Aunt Caroline had been fond of pronouncing, "are the devil's invention." And she'd been right, Kim decided, hauling forth the large flat carton she'd stowed at the back of the front hall closet more than a week ago. Sitting around wallowing in her misfortunes would do nothing but add to her lengthy list of miseries, and pacing the floor would merely wear out the rug. If she couldn't discipline herself to be creative, she could tackle something mechanical.

"U-Assemble," the directions stated. "No special tools required." Easy enough, she thought, and a worthy project to keep her hands and mind occupied on such a dreadful day. She would put together the sturdy wooden wagon she'd bought Jason for Christmas.

It was an irreproachable gift, sensible, indestructible, versatile, educational even, if the manufacturer's claims were to be believed. Jason could tow it behind him, ride in it, sit in it, pile it high with sand or toys. Adam could not possibly fault her choice. And as a gesture of independence, she would fill it with designer jeans and T-shirts before she deposited it under the Christmas tree.

Two hours later, frustrated and defeated, surrounded by an assortment of pieces that clearly required advanced engineering skills to make sense out of them, she leaned her head on the cushions of her couch and gave in to the despair that had been compounded by her morning's activities.

"Nothing," she wailed to the room at large, "ever seems to work the way I planned."

"Which way's that?" Adam's voice inquired. "And why are you kneeling on the floor surrounded by all that mess?"

He stood in the doorway leading to the kitchen, shaking the rain from his oilskin jacket. "I came in the back way so I wouldn't drip on the rug," he explained sheepishly. "And when you didn't hear me knocking, I let myself in."

Speechless, she stared up at him, horribly conscious of her shiny nose and unbrushed hair.

"Is there something wrong, Kim?"

That he should even have to ask! "Everything," she uttered hoarsely.

He strolled over to where she still knelt, his mouth twitching and his eyes silvering with amusement. "So what are you doing about it?" he asked. "Praying?"

Why was it, she wondered dismally, that when she was most in need of a little pampering, he saw fit to dispense nothing but humor or sarcasm? She waved a dispirited hand around. "This," she informed him, "is Jason's Christmas gift."

"Good Lord." Adam sank to one knee, laughter rippling through his words. "What was it?"

"You might well ask. I should have stuck to what I know I can do and not tried to please you."

"Is that what you were trying to do? Please me?"

"I'm always trying to please you, and Jason, and I'm always failing."

"My, my," Adam chided her gently. "Aren't we feeling sorry for ourselves this morning!"

She pushed herself back on her heels and eased herself up to the couch, determined not to reproach him with her large, injured eyes. If he wanted to forget last night, she wasn't going to bring it up. "Not in the slightest," she retorted. "But it's easy for you to talk. You don't have to prove yourself to anyone."

"Except myself."

"Which I'm sure isn't difficult." She massaged her aching legs. All that kneeling had just about crippled her. "Considering how much Jason loves you. Is that why you always do everything just right around him, and I make so many mistakes?"

He looked at her curiously. "I thought I had you convinced that no one's perfect, not even me. I make mistakes all the time, just as you do."

"But Jason adores you."

"I wouldn't go that far, but I think he knows he can count on me, that I'll always be there for him. More to the point, though, is that you come to see what you've given him, too."

"Yes," she replied bitterly, "I have a marvelous track record, haven't I? The kite, the designer originals, the—"

"Dammit, Kim, stop belittling yourself. You know full well I'm not talking about *things*. What about all the love you have to give, all the time and patience? Don't they count for more than that?"

"You really believe I have those to give?" Her eyes were pure gold fringed in smoky lashes, as wide and startled as a doe's. He wanted to gather her into his arms and chase the undermining doubts away, to bring her out into the sunshine of her own worth.

"Oh, yes," he said. "All that and more. I think that what you have to give Jason from your heart adds up to a greater gift than anything else you could possibly think of."

"Sometimes," she said, her voice tremulous with tearful joy, "you say the nicest things."

"Sometimes," he told her, leaning forward and kissing the tip of her shiny nose with all the affection of a brother, "you deserve them. Now make us some coffee, and I'll help you assemble this . . . thing."

She paused on her way to the kitchen, unable to help herself from voicing the one question that all her intuition told her should remain unasked. "What brought you over here today, Adam?"

He glanced up from reading the directions for the wagon. She had an unbearably expectant look, he saw, that stirred to life all the tenderness that had led him astray last night. What could he say to her? "Thank you for letting me be the first to make love to you"?

He'd thought he knew her; he'd thought for weeks that she'd been playing some complicated game whose rules only she knew. Last night . . . Hell, why had he let last night happen? She'd been an innocent, a virgin. Whatever her game, she wasn't playing fair and he didn't know what to make of her—or of himself.

"I wanted to make sure you were okay." His gaze caught and locked with hers. She thought she saw regret there and felt the quiet death of all her hopes. "And I brought over a decent flashlight. If this weather keeps up, the power lines could come down at any time, and you'll need more than a couple of candles to keep you going."

"I see." She swallowed her disappointment. "Thanks for thinking of it."

Even with a fire roaring up the chimney and her favorite record of the Boston Philharmonic spilling into every corner of the house, the grayness outside seemed to seep through the walls to permeate her spirits. Afternoon slipped imperceptibly into dusk with no abatement in the storm, and when, shortly before seven o'clock, the power once again fell victim to the weather, the independence she'd sworn to adopt earlier evaporated as reminders of the previous night rushed in on her.

Stumbling miserably around in the dark, she realized she had no clear idea of just where Adam had placed the flashlight, and the only candles in the house were upstairs, right where he'd left them. By the glow of the dying fire, she climbed the stairs in Muldoon's energetic wake and groped her way to the bedroom. How utterly black the room was with not even the illuminated dial of the clock to cast its dim green light.

She was feeling her way to the bedside table when it happened. There was a groaning roar that split the night with such force that the storm paled to mere background accompaniment by comparison, and then the whole house shuddered.

Oh, God! she thought in terror. It's an earthquake!

Cold air gusted around her, increasing her panic, and she scrambled onto the high bed as something across the room crashed to the floor. The dreaded aftershocks had begun, the house was collapsing, and she was going to be buried alive in the rubble.

The very thought snagged the air in her lungs and jolted her into action. Leaping from the bed, she stumbled wildly to the door and wrenched on the handle.

Nothing—absolutely nothing—happened. The door might have been a part of the wall for all that it yielded to her puny strength. It was jammed solid and she was trapped. Panic-stricken, she pounded the sturdy wood and yanked futilely on the porcelain handle.

From the other side, Muldoon scratched at the door, whining anxiously, then suddenly gave two short, excited barks. In the same instant, Kim thought she heard voices. "Help!" she yelled, fear lending her unexpected lung power.

Unidentified footsteps, more than one pair, sounded below her in the living room, but the voice that reached up the stairs was one she'd have recognized anywhere. "Kim, where are you?"

"Adam! Up here!"

She heard him race up the stairs, she heard the solid thud of his shoulder against the door, and then she felt relief flood her with weakness. He was here and he'd defy anything nature could invent in order to save her.

"The door's jammed on your side," he shouted. "What's holding it back?"

"I don't know," she wailed. "I can't see a thing."

"Use the flashlight," he suggested reasonably.

"I can't. I don't have it." Claustrophobia was creeping up on her, making her voice all wobbly.

There was a second's silence, then he spoke again, striving, she could tell, for patience. "Do you have candles, then?"

"I don't know where you left them," she said pitifully. "They're not by the bed anymore."

Out on the landing, Adam felt Tom Baxter's speculative gaze skate over him, then slide hurriedly off into space as Adam impaled him with a glare. "They're on the dresser," he said shortly, his eyes steadfastly daring Tom to betray a speck of curiosity. "By the door."

Inside the room, Kim groped over to where her antique chiffonier should have been and encountered only empty space. Maybe she had misjudged the distance, she thought, and stepped incautiously forward, only to bark her shins painfully on the edge of something hard—the frame of the mirror atop the dresser, she recognized, her fingers tracing its carved surface. "Adam," she called, "the chiffonier's fallen over and it's blocking the door."

His heart had almost stopped with fear when he'd realized she was up in the bedroom, then raced like a windup toy when he heard her voice and knew she was alive; and now, irrationally, he was flooded with anger. That damned great ugly eyesore of a dresser was preventing him from getting her out of this miserable little house and into the safety of his arms. Impotently, he smashed a fist against the wall and let fly with a string of curses that had Tom's eyebrows jumping sky-high.

"Judge?"

Adam glowered. "We'll have to break the damned door down, Tom." He raised his voice. "You hear that, Kim? Stand well back. We're coming in."

One well-aimed kick demolished the old latch, and after that, they made short work of stripping the door from its hinges. Shoving it aside, Adam grabbed his flashlight and climbed through the space, unceremoniously planting his heavy boots on the polished wood of the dresser.

She was crouched on the bed, unhurt and indignant, her pupils enormous and ringed in amber, and he was suddenly drenched in a cold sweat. If she'd been hurt— killed . . .

His thoughts sheared away, unable to cope with the idea. The savagery of the night, he realized dimly, would have been no match for the black depths of his grief and loss. "You're okay," he said, the words a marvel of understatement overlaid with husky relief. His eyes swept over her, clung to her.

Why didn't he rush over and grab her in his arms? she wondered, then saw Tom hovering to the rear and sensed that Adam would not display any such overt affection in front of the other man. No, indeed, she thought bitterly. She was something he liked to fool around with only in private. He'd made that clear enough last night on the beach.

She felt suddenly naked, meeting his silver gray gaze across the width of the disordered bed. Last night, it had been— Oh, hell! What was the point in harping on what had happened last night? He certainly wasn't back in her bedroom now for a repeat performance. "I'm fine," she replied coolly, "which is more than can be said for my chiffonier. Look at what you've done to it!"

His eyes filmed red with rage. *"What?"*

She quaked at his tone and averted her gaze. "Well, it's very old and deserves to be treated with more reverence. It belonged to my Great-granduncle Samuel. He was a sea captain and he brought it back—"

"I don't give a damn," he ground out, "if it belonged to the Queen of Sheba."

"Obviously not," she retorted. "You just tromped all

over it." She climbed down from the bed. "Tom," she cooed, smiling winningly at the man as he lingered uncertainly in the splintered doorway, "will you help me set it upright?"

"Never mind the bloody furniture." Adam reached out and manacled her wrist. "We're getting out of here now."

"Let me go," she commanded imperiously. "I'm not going anywhere. The earthquake's over."

"Earthquake? That was no earthquake." He spat out a mirthless laugh and pointed to the ceiling. "Take a look up there," he advised. "That monstrous cedar on the west side came down on your roof and made a hole you could drive a car through."

"Oh, for heaven's sake . . ." She made to grab the flashlight he held. "We've got to protect the furniture from the rain."

"Forget it." If possible, he clamped his fingers even more securely around her wrist. "The furniture'll have to fend for itself until daylight. We won't know the extent of the damage until then."

"But the bedspread . . ." She almost squawked in her indignation. "The chiffonier . . . the bed! Be serious. I can't leave them unprotected."

He compressed his lips in undisguised exasperation. She could be the most maddening creature when the mood took her, and he was in no shape to put up with any more of her nonsense tonight. Good Lord, had she no idea how badly he'd been frightened by her plight? "You can and you will. Get a coat and a pair of boots and put that hysterical hound on a leash."

Muldoon, apparently pixilated by the weather, was careening around in ever-diminishing circles in pursuit of his own tail.

"Whatever for? I'm not going to walk him tonight."

"Tom, check that the power's off at the main box and see that the front door's locked. And you"—Adam turned back to Kim—"tell me what you need in the way

130

of clothes and . . . stuff . . . for the next couple of days."

"I will not." Did he think he was her lord and master just because he'd seduced her? "Not until you tell me why."

At Adam's indrawn breath and tongue-clicking annoyance, Tom broke in. "You'll have to leave the house, miss. It's not safe."

"Not safe how?"

"The roof could give . . . The tree may only have come part way down, and the rest could follow . . . There could be live wires down . . . Any number of things. We won't know until we can examine it in daylight, and if this weather keeps up, we won't be able to get a really good look for some time."

"But the furniture and paintings . . . the rugs . . ." She was appalled. All her treasured heirlooms in danger of ruination. "I can't just abandon them."

Adam gave a snort of pure frustration. "Woman," he ground out, the light of battle in his gunmetal eyes apparent even by flashlight, "you are enough to try the patience of a saint. And I," he threatened, advancing on her menacingly, "am merely a man, one perilously close to the end of my tether."

Oh, he was a man, all right, every last masculine inch of him, and no "merely" about it!

"Don't smirk at me!" he thundered, sending Tom into near seizures of embarrassment. "Are you going to tell me what clothes you want, or not?"

"Not," she retorted. "I'll get them myself." Sometimes, he was too overbearing to be borne, not to mention righteous and stuffy.

"Over my dead body," he replied.

She stopped on her way to the stairs and tossed him a defiant glance. "Don't bully me, Adam. You don't own me, despite what you may think. This is still my house, even with part of the roof missing, and I can do as I please, without your permission."

"One more step, Kim," he promised her, "one more, and I'll paddle your behind till you can't sit down. And that, madam, is no idle threat."

He meant every word, she realized, taking note of his sober expression. He actually would carry out his threat, in front of Tom, if need be. Good grief! "Very well," she conceded graciously, some devil of mischief taking possession of her tongue. "I need a nightgown and a robe, some lingerie and panty hose. Oh, and my worsted gray pantsuit and the striped silk blouse—they're both in the left-hand side of the burled walnut armoire—and my black mohair sweater, which is in the cedar closet in the hall. And then I guess I'll need—"

"You'll need a pair of jeans and a warm sweater," Adam cut in. "You're taking temporary refuge, not moving in permanently."

"—something for dinner. Perhaps my black silk dress," she persisted saucily. "You'll know it when you see it, I'm sure. And my toothbrush and my hairbrush and, heavens, yes, my dental floss. Mustn't let anything get in the way of flossing every day."

"Keep it up," Adam warned her. "Just keep it up and the only thing you'll need is a cushion for your backside."

"I'm cringing at the mere thought," she snapped. "Now, if you'll kindly step aside, I'll go get a few essentials to see me through tomorrow."

"I'll take the dog over to the kennel," Tom interjected hurriedly, looping his belt through Muldoon's collar and preparing to beat a hasty retreat onto the porch and out into the wild night.

"Take her. I'll bring the dog," Adam commanded, grasping Kim ungently about the upper arm and steering her toward the door.

"Miss?" Tom peered at her apologetically as he held

out his hand. "Let me help you with a coat and something for your feet. Please?"

"Oh . . ." Frustration in every line of her body, Kim swung back to Adam. "Dirty pool," she accused him, "*very* dirty pool." How could she defy him if it meant exposing nice Tom Baxter to his employer's wrath?

"Don't waste time, Tom," Adam ordered implacably. "And leave me the big flashlight. I'll need it to go looking for Ms. Forester's . . . essentials."

"I'll bring my own dog," Kim asserted, taking a last pathetic stab at independence. "I wouldn't dream of leaving him to your mercy."

"As you wish—but get on with it."

"Yes, sir, Your Honor!" She prepared to saunter out, dumb insolence in her every leisurely step, but the sudden tension in Adam's body, accompanied by the weighty displeasure in his regard, dissuaded her. She left in undignified haste, thoroughly put to rout by his glacial outrage.

CHAPTER TEN

The sour aftertaste of fear lingering in his throat had made him unnecessarily curt with her, he knew. And she'd responded just as he should have expected, rearing up in affronted pride as though he were still the stranger from next door and her enemy. Had last night been so distasteful to her?

He climbed the stairs, his jaw clenched in irritation. He'd never understand her. She'd practically invited him to seduce her, sparing no thought for how he felt about divesting her of her virginity without grace or patience. Then, when he'd tried to atone for his haste, and brought her to a realization of fulfillment, she'd turned inexplicably petulant.

Hounded by guilt and concern, he'd come back this afternoon and been confronted with a woman whose vulnerability had stripped him bare, and only then had he realized the enormity of what had transpired the night before. Walking away from this warm, generous woman who gave of herself with such passion was not something he would easily be able to do. He was involved, whether he liked it or not. And now, just when he thought he had the whole picture in focus, she reverted to type, obsessed with her damned possessions and maintaining her precious status quo.

Propping the flashlight on the edge of the infamous chiffonier, he pulled open the top drawer and was at once entrapped in the elusive scent of her that swirled around him and made a mockery of his anger. The drawer was filled with soft, silky things—bits of lace and wisps of satin designed, surely, to drive a man to madness, for they were too insubstantial to serve any more utilitarian purpose.

He riffled his fingers through the neat layers, appalled at the shaft of desire that pierced him. The flimsy garments were as smooth and caressing as her skin, tantalizing him with their intimate knowledge of her body. He crushed the gossamer fabric in his hands, his mind awash with erotic visions.

He was past redemption. Grimly, he searched for something plain and unadorned and had to content himself with a pair of ecru bikini panties beguilingly edged with French lace. Frothy and irreverent, they clung to his fingers, and he shook them roughly into a heap next to the flashlight, slammed closed the drawer, and drew open the next, only to close it, too, with a force that paid scant respect to its antiquity. He was not about to start foraging among the dainty brief cups that posed as her bras. It was asking too much of any man.

Her night wear nestled in the fourth drawer, some satin and silk, beribboned and bedecked with seduction in mind, others demure and chaste, an invitation to plunder the treasures they were designed to disguise. Did she own a single thing that wasn't aimed at reducing him to a quivering heap of pubescent lust? He fumbled for something—anything—and closed his fingers blindly on some garment and flung it atop the underwear, refusing to torment himself further, then turned his back and strode savagely to the armoire.

Even by flashlight, he could see his distorted reflection in the satin sheen of the wood. It was probably another priceless heirloom, although when he was a boy, it would have been called a wardrobe and would have been disposed of in favor of something sleek and cheap and modern. Only after his father had made his fortune had the

135

Ryans aspired to anything as grandiose as the rich life-style to which Kim had been born. By then, Adam had put himself through law school, working summers in remote logging camps and evenings in the campus cafeteria, and had no need of the money that flowed so freely through his father's fingers.

Jocelyn, of course, had been another matter entirely. At age nine, she'd been inundated with things—toys, clothes, parties, a pony; anything and everything that had captured her fancy. She was overindulged to make up for the parental neglect to which she fell victim—and hopelessly headstrong. And look where it had all ended.

The anger flared again. What was it about women that they were ready to forfeit life itself for the cheap thrills of material possessions? First, his mother, abdicating all responsibility for the daughter she'd borne, too busy with her tardily acquired clubs and charities to have time to shape a young girl's values. Then Jocelyn, tossing life away when it had scarcely begun, bored by it all. Now Kim, willful and obsessed, more concerned with her bloody antiques than she was with her own safety.

Yet how could he maintain his well-founded disapproval of her actions when the mere mention of her name incited him to heights of desire he'd never before permitted? He was enslaved, reduced to a level he despised.

Defeated, he searched out the jeans and sweater he'd originally intended to collect, swept up the items on the chiffonier, and stuffed the lot into the suede tote bag he'd found in the bottom of the armoire. Taking rapid inventory of the bathroom, he collected her toothbrush, her hairbrush, and in a moment of weakness, a small bottle of perfume.

If anything, the storm had worsened, the wind screaming across the ocean in demented gusts, making it impossible to ascertain the damage inflicted on her house. He'd known that tree was unsafe; he had berated Greg about it.

"Take the damn thing down before someone gets killed," he'd barked. "Cedars have no tap roots, anyone'll tell you that."

Typically, Greg had ignored the warning, but that scarcely exonerated Adam. That he'd intended to act on the matter himself, after Kim arrived, was little comfort. Good intentions were a poor substitute for actions at the best of times, as well he knew. His guilt at not having attempted to change the course of Jocelyn's life was burden enough, and one he'd had a hard time accepting. To have exposed Kim's life to danger was unforgivable.

He and Tom had been making their way up the bluff to the cottage, bringing her extra lamps to see her through the power cut that could, Adam knew, last for hours in a storm like this. Fear had paralyzed him, drenching him in a chilling sweat, and left a raw and bitter taste in his mouth when he'd heard the tree come down. He'd recognized the sound, the reverberating impact, immediately. No one who'd worked the logging camps could mistake it. He'd seen a man crushed to a pulp by a felled pine. Tonight, in the instant before he'd been galvanized by panic, he'd had a sudden vision of Kim pinned beneath the deadly limbs of the cedar and hadn't recognized as his own the hoarse cry of horror that had echoed above the storm. He knew now that the anger he'd experienced since had been conjured up solely to hold at bay that awful fear—and the disquieting conclusions it had forced him to confront.

"She's relaxing in a hot tub," Claudia Baxter informed him as he appeared, somewhat wild-eyed, in the hallway leading to the main staircase. "Then she's coming down to join you for a nightcap. Tom's started a fire in the living room."

"What about her clothes? They must be soaked from the rain."

"It's all taken care of, Judge." The housekeeper cast him a questioning glance. "Are you all right?"

"Sorry, Mrs. B." He collected himself with an effort. "I guess I'm more shaken up by what happened than I realized. Tom, too, I imagine. Bring a tray of sandwiches and coffee to the living room, then look after Tom. He's earned a bit of extra attention."

Adam turned away, increasingly dismayed at the unmanageability of his thoughts. His concern, his fear, and his anger, in company with the powerful attraction he felt for Kim, added up to a good deal more than a sensuous romp between scented sheets. The last he'd enjoyed with a number of discreet women, and he knew the game too well not to recognize that this time the rules were different. The perennial bachelor was in danger of falling victim to an unpredictable little madam who was managing to disrupt his entire life-style.

The fire blazed in the hearth, and twin oil lamps cast a mellow light over the gracious room. The velvet drapes were drawn against the wild weather, a decanter of his best cognac waited on a beaten brass tray on a side table —and there he was, a man old enough to know better, pacing the floor like an anxious swain from some melodramatic musical comedy. The door should open any minute now to admit the heroine, swathed in chiffon and a feather boa.

Mrs. Baxter appeared instead. "Here are the sandwiches, Judge, and a pot of hot chocolate. No coffee, I'm afraid, till the electricity's restored, but I managed to heat some milk over the kitchen fire."

"That's fine, Mrs. B. Probably better for us, in fact. Just leave it and we'll help ourselves later."

He poked at the wood on the fire and glanced at his watch. He was wound up as tight as a spring; he needed something to distract him, to release the tension coiling inside. How long could a bath take? She must have been upstairs close to an hour.

Crossing the room, he lifted the lid to the grand piano and, sliding onto the bench, flung himself into an impassioned rendition of Rachmaninoff's Piano Concerto no. 2 in C Minor. It never failed, he thought fifteen minutes later as the relief inched down his neck and across his shoulders. Relaxing, he allowed his fingers to drift over the keys, picking out snatches of melody before falling into an old familiar love song.

The bath did more than refresh Kim. It washed away the resentment and left behind regret that she'd lacked the grace or intelligence to see his actions for what they were: concern for her and valid recognition of the potential danger of the situation. That she should have elected to assert her independence at such a time was misguided, to say the least.

Ashamed, she stepped from the tub and dried herself, then pulled on the blue velour robe Claudia had loaned her. Buttoning it from her throat to her knees, she glanced in the mirror and pushed her hair roughly into shape. For once, appearances must take second place.

She started down the stairs in bare feet, resolved to make an apology to Adam. That she could do so over tonight's events, when pride had kept her silent over other things, told her much. What would have struck her as an admission of inexcusable weakness two months ago seemed now a display of strength that she prayed would survive his justified annoyance.

The sound of the piano, hauntingly romantic, lured her silently from the foot of the stairs and across the hall to the living room doorway. She knew that song. It was from an old thirties musical she'd seen revived in an off-Broadway production two years ago.

Adam sat at the keys, his back to her, and even in the shadows cast by the oil lamps and the fire, she could sense his weariness. The shoulders she'd never seen other than wide and willing to carry the burdens of the whole world were slumped, and all her finely rehearsed words of apology died unuttered, chased away by a remorse so intense that it pained her.

The song was a magnet, drawing her to him until she was into the room and leaning against the mirrored finish of the grand piano. Without stopping to consider the enormity of her actions, she fitted the words to the melody he played in her husky, slightly off-key contralto. " 'Won't you please take a chance on a lifetime romance . . . with me . . .' "

There was a brief hesitation in his hands, a scarcely perceptible halt to the rhythm, as he lifted his head and met her gaze. Did he see the tenderness and regret there? " 'I gave you my heart, right at the start, gave you . . . all of me . . .' "

She wouldn't look away; she wouldn't deny him this one glimpse of all she had hidden in her heart. He might not want to see, he might turn from her, but she wouldn't be the one to back away from the truth this time. " 'I dream night and day, keep hoping we may have a . . . lifetime . . . romance . . .' "

Oh, it wasn't so easy, after all, to bare her soul and leave it unprotected to his indifference. She couldn't finish—she couldn't get the last words past the constriction in her throat. But he held her prisoner in his gaze, neither blinking nor breathing, it seemed. Just waiting . . . waiting, only his fingers, independent of the rest of him, moving ruthlessly to the closing bars.

" 'There's no more to say . . . Not a thing I can do, but' "—she swallowed—" 'tell you . . . the truth . . .' "

Such pain, such fear, such awful dread! She'd never said the words to any man and they terrified her. The notes fell slowly, relentlessly, dragging the admission past her unwilling lips. " 'I'm . . . in love' "—at the last, her eyes fell closed—" 'with . . . you.' "

She thought the utter stillness of the room would

smother her. Drawing in shallow, desperate breaths, she fled, back up the stairs, away from the unremitting scrutiny of his fathomless gray gaze.

It meant nothing, he told himself as the silence came crashing down in the wake of her departure. It was a song, nothing more. And he needed a drink, badly.

He strode to the tray and splashed cognac into a snifter. She was playing games again, his mind warned him. Adopting another role—as if he weren't confounded enough. Lord, how many were there? Aunt, siren, innocent, brat—and now, the coup de grace: lover more tender than springtime. Would the real Kim Forester please step forward!

He raised his glass to the light and watched the rich topaz liquid tilt and cling to the crystal, made to toss the brandy down his throat, and stopped. It was a crying shame to abuse fine cognac this way. It deserved to be savored, rolled gently along the tongue and over the palate. Like Kim. Surrendering to the urge that had gnawed at him for hours, he measured an inch of liquor into a second snifter and, cradling both in one hand, followed her up the stairs.

He had not, she thought heatedly, a romantic bone in his body. Look at his choice of clothes for her: jeans, a sweater, fresh underwear. *Sensible.*

Then the last item spilled out, and she was completely floored at his selection of night wear. Of all the bedroom attire she possessed, from cotton nightshirts to full-length and sober flannel gowns, what in the world had prompted him to select this particular garment? And wrapped around a bottle of her favorite perfume, yet.

Walking to the mirrored closet, she shed Claudia's robe and held the brief item against her naked body. Peach satin, appliquéd with lace, the hem and cuffs edged with marabou, it served neither as gown nor peignoir, and why

141

should it? It was the top half of a pair of lounging pajamas and by itself very suggestive. Perhaps her roundabout admission of love had not been so misguided, after all. Both she and Adam seemed more comfortable with the indirect approach, for there was surely a message behind his choice of night wear for her.

She sprayed the air with perfume, absorbing its fragrance into her skin and hair, then slid the cool folds of satin over her shoulders. He couldn't possibly have known that what he'd selected would be so . . . abbreviated. When she dropped her arms to her sides, the cuffs hung lower than the hem.

She had just finished tying the laces that held the front closed when the knock came discreetly at her door. Oh, she'd surmised correctly. He had meant something in choosing the pajama top. But what if it weren't he? Suppose it were Claudia or, perish the thought, Tom?

Clutching the top modestly to her, she opened the door a mere crack and pressed her eye to the opening, then gasped in surprise and pain as the door swung open, grazing roughly across the tops of her toes. She hopped from one foot to the other, unmindful of her guest or the need to subdue the upheaval of rippling satin, her eyes stinging from the sharp impact to her feet. Good grief, but that hurt!

By the time her vision had cleared, it was too late for second thoughts or second-guessing. Adam was in the room, the door was closed again, and the air was suddenly humming with a tension that had nothing to do with regret or modesty.

He swallowed twice and reached behind him to deposit the brandy snifters on a nearby table. She was wearing the same perfume, more pervasive than it had been in her dresser drawers, and very little else.

"You're staring, Adam," she informed him softly.

He swallowed again. "Small wonder. Where on earth did you get that thing?"

142

"This?" She peered at him teasingly from under lowered lashes and pirouetted daintily, the marabou flaring out, then subsiding in caressing little eddies against the smooth skin of her thighs. She hadn't missed his unguarded response to her appearance, and hope reborn surged through her. Surely he cared for her, too, at least a little?

"Kim"—Adam held a hand to his forehead and closed his eyes—"don't do that." The flash of golden flesh, the sweet curves and shadowed hollows undulating beneath the glossy fabric, sent his senses swirling. He wanted to make slow, delicious love to her—and feared he might fling her to the floor and ravish her.

She laughed and stepped closer, the feathered trim of her top brushing against his denim-clad thighs with devastating effect. "Oh, Adam, you know very well where this came from."

"Kim"—he held her at a safe distance, striving to maintain an even tone despite the warm velvet of her bare skin beneath his hands—"play fair. Better yet, stop playing altogether. I'm not made of stone, nor am I in the mood for a repeat of last night's abuse."

Uncertainty came flooding back. Withering with shame at her brazen behavior, she retreated into offended dignity, determined to conceal the extent of her dismay. "If you don't want to seduce me, then what do you mean by sneaking up here like this?"

Hurt and confusion were mirrored in her clear gaze, and he cursed his clumsiness, wishing just once that they could react to each other without the suspicion and sensitivity to slight that seemed to shadow their every exchange. "I didn't sneak in," he reminded her gently. "I knocked at the door, and you opened it and let me in."

"I did no such thing!" She held the hem of her top firmly to her thighs and prayed that the lacing that held the front together hadn't come untied. "I didn't know it was you outside."

143

"Really?" A slow smile warmed his face as his eyes caressed her, and for all that she fought to subdue it, excitement pricked along the backs of her knees. "Then who were you expecting?"

"Mrs. Baxter," she lied faintly.

"Dressed like that?" He reached out and wound the laces around the fingers of one hand. Faced with the choice of resisting him and having the top pulled undone, she yielded to the gentle tug and found herself pressed against him. "What a terrible waste," he murmured, his breath rippling over her hair and face.

"Adam . . . what if—"

"No one will," he whispered. "They wouldn't dare." His lips nibbled at her mouth with demoralizing thoroughness, and the prickling behind her knees spread and threatened to seize her in uncontrolled spasms of bliss.

"You must think I'm putty in your hands," she gasped in a last futile effort at restraint.

"Oh, darling," he breathed, and her head swam with dizzying rapture at the endearment. He brought both arms around her and ran his hands from the nape of her neck to the base of her spine, letting his fingers spread to cup the soft fullness of her rounded derriere. "Oh, darling," he repeated huskily, "putty is the last thing on my mind."

With consummate skill, he explored the line of her jaw, the curve of her ear, and the arch of her neck with his tongue, meanwhile driving her to distraction with the slow stroking of the long, elegant fingers that had woven such magic at the keyboard. She felt the last pitiful shreds of her resistance collapse, and uttering a soft, despairing groan, she buried her face in his shoulder and let her arms steal around his waist. What other choice did she have when her body was edging toward that erotic other planet where time and reason faded and only the immediacy of his flesh against hers counted?

The marabou swirled between them, teasing the full

144

urgency of his hunger like a thousand fleeting fingers. The naked silk of her skin vied with the gleaming satin of the pajama top, gold overlaid with ripe peach, a feast too rich for his eyes alone. He had to touch, to taste. He had to possess her again and again—perhaps forever.

The bed was soft and inviting. He sank down with her in the cool sheets, plying her with fervent sweet kisses, and she returned them with uninhibited abandon, caring not at all that the satin top had slipped aside, revealing all but the topmost curve of her breasts.

Lowering his head, Adam pressed his lips to her neck, then sought the laces that were valiantly defending the tattered remains of her modesty. Taking one delicate strand between his teeth, he tugged it free of its neighbor and, with a hot, persistent tongue, defined each full and aching breast, each bold and rosy nipple.

"Oh . . . please . . ." she whispered, echoes of last night's cascading passion rippling distantly along her nerves.

He needed no second bidding. Stripping off his clothes, he stretched out beside her and let the subtle promise of his tongue and the gentle persuasion of his fingers lead her again to the brink of rapture. Only then did he allow the wild exuberant joy to run free, to soar between them, to permeate his soul and hers, and finally, to ebb to a pale shadow of ecstasy.

And in the sweet aftermath of loving her, he surprised himself by turning her face up to his and letting the unplanned admission escape him. "I love you," he said. Even as he spoke the words, he was shattered and appalled because it was true and had been for weeks.

Her eyes grew wide and luminous. "Really?" she whispered. "I mean, *really?* Not just because we . . . you know . . ."

Yes, he really did, for all kinds of crazy reasons, including the ongoing battle between her puritan sense of what was proper and her flagrantly responsive body.

Covering his mouth with his hand, he attempted to wipe away the grin that threatened to mar his features and failed completely. "What?" he teased her. "Go on, say it."

"Don't you dare laugh," she warned him, scowling ferociously. "Not tonight, not about something this serious."

"Yes, ma'am."

"Please," she begged, "I can't bear to have you joke about it."

"Oh, honey," he protested, seeing the insecurity that lurked ready to pounce on the tentative joy in her gaze, "don't you know there's something rather special about two people being able to laugh in bed? Where is it written that lovemaking has to be so solemn?"

She regarded him gravely. "You're a solemn sort of person," she informed him. "I get very uneasy when you suddenly become flighty and frivolous—in bed or out."

He hooted at her choice of words. May God forgive him, he couldn't help himself. He'd been called a lot of things in his time, but *flighty* and *frivolous* weren't two of them.

"This isn't funny," she scolded him.

He caught her to him and scattered kisses over her hair and face. "I know," he replied penitently. "It's wonderful and special—like you."

"And serious?"

He kissed the tip of her nose. "Definitely. I wouldn't lie about something like this. I've never told a woman I loved her before. It's not something to be taken lightly."

"Oh, good!" She sagged against him in relief and turned her head to provide his lips with fuller access to her neck. "Everything's going to work out the way I hoped, after all."

"How so?" he murmured, nuzzling the pad of her earlobe.

"Well, for a start, no more battles over where Jason belongs."

Adam's tongue, about to taste the perfumed hollow behind her ear, withdrew to run thoughtfully over his lower lip. "Yes . . . that would be nice."

"Yes." She stretched luxuriously and tucked herself more firmly to him. "He'll have both of us now."

"That's true," Adam replied cautiously. "And has been for some time."

"Oh, but Adam"—she tilted up her head and offered him her mouth, her lips, swollen from his kisses, curved in a smile so radiant it almost hurt to witness it—"we can be together now, just like a normal family."

Was it mere moments ago that he'd been regretting the undercurrents that tainted everything between them? "A normal family," he repeated reflectively. "Tell me, how did you arrive at—"

"We could adopt him, couldn't we—after we get married, of course?"

Suspicion crystallized into certainty laced with a strange, hurting anger. "Who said anything about marriage?" he inquired coolly, feeling a perverse satisfaction in seeing the shock that widened her slumberous gold gaze.

She was mortified, terrified even, at the way her tongue had run away with her. "Oh," she murmured lightly, tracing the fine hair that curled across his chest with a dainty fingertip, and praying he wouldn't detect her inner trembling, "it just seemed the most sensible solution, that's all." *Sensible.* That was the word to emphasize. Adam was greatly impressed by anything sensible.

He removed her hand. "Solution? I wasn't aware we had a problem. Explain it to me."

She pulled away from him. "Well, it's better for any child to have two parents, and naturally, I just assumed when you said you loved me—"

"A sentiment I'm living to regret, and one that you

147

seem curiously reluctant to echo," he returned bitterly, hardening his heart at the anguish that swept over her features.

"No!" she insisted, reaching out and cupping his cheek tenderly. "I told you downstairs. Of course I love you. Why else"—she withdrew her hand and held it palm uppermost to give the words emphasis—"why else would I want to marry you?"

"Oh," he replied with brutal candor, "I can think of a number of reasons that have nothing at all to do with your feelings for me." He laced his fingers behind his head and stared across the room. "For example, you get Jason without losing face in another messy court battle—which, incidentally, you'd never win. You get to exercise your questionable influence over him during his formative years. You also get the respectability of marriage, something that I suspect is a lot more important to you than the husband who provides it. In short, my darling little manipulator, you get what you've been after since the day you first got here."

"What?" She was aghast.

"Yes," he nodded. "I haven't forgotten the night you wore the black dress, remember? You as good as admitted you were out to trap me then. And last night: 'Take me home, Adam. Let's be alone, Adam.' More of the same, my darling."

Oh, the irony in the endearment, turning it into a scathing condemnation of her integrity and worth. She felt her heart wither. "You can't believe that was all a calculated effort on my part," she implored him, denying what was so clearly evident in the shuttered expression of his face, the remote gray light of his eyes. "How can you say you love me and even *think* such things?"

"How can I not?" he returned, shifting his gaze to rake over her as he reached down beside the bed for his pants. "Hell, you've got it all worked out. I can practically see the canary feathers sticking out the corners of your mouth. The cat just bagged another trophy, right?"

She wanted to cry, to howl with pain and misery and disappointment, and somehow managed to dam up the tears in her throat, remaining dry-eyed but inarticulate. He pulled on his shirt and tucked it into his jeans, casually zipped up the fly, then picked up his shoes and turned to the door. He was walking out of the room and out of her life, and she was desperate to halt the inevitability of it all.

"What if someone sees you leaving here?" she asked him, despising the beseeching whine in her voice.

"What if they do?" he returned indifferently. "It's my house. I can do as I please."

Reviving anger engulfed her. Oh, he was a heartless snake, insufferably arrogant! How dare he just pick up and leave like this? "Not with me, you can't. Don't think, just because I love you, that I'll let you walk all over me. I'll sue for custody." Such wild, foolish threats, but how else could she prevent herself from falling into a disgusting, soggy, hysterical heap on the bed? How in the world had everything changed so drastically, all their tender, searing passion obliterated in bitter accusations and misunderstandings?

"See you in court," he replied laconically, and put his hand on the doorknob.

"No! Adam, please!" She was off the bed in a flash, still naked, the sheets trailing behind her. "I didn't mean that." She grasped the steel that was his arm in both hands, unashamedly pleading. "I want to marry you because I love you. All the rest is just . . . extra. What's so wrong with that? Isn't love what marriage is all about?" She shook his unresponsive flesh. "Isn't it?"

He fixed his cool, appraising glance on her flushed face, then dropped it to the fingers clutching his arm. Dismayed, she let him go, recognizing her utter failure to convince him of her sincerity.

149

"I see," she said quietly. "You don't want to believe me, do you? You'd never even considered marriage, had you?"

Marriage? Hell, he hadn't even known he loved her until tonight, let alone think about marrying her. But she'd obviously thought about it a great deal; she had been waiting for the chance to maneuver him into it, in fact. And he'd set himself up, given her the perfect opening. He felt like a jackass, all his earlier distrust of her resurfacing, dulling for now the aching pain in his heart. How come, at his age and with his experience, he was up to his knees in alligators before he realized he was caught in a swamp? "Why, Kim," he returned gently, "I didn't have to consider anything. You did the thinking for both of us."

He opened the door. "Pity I can't accept your proposal, but I don't like the motives that prompted it."

"I didn't—" she began, then stopped. No need to advertise their disagreement to the whole house. "I did *not* propose," she whispered indignantly. "I made an unfortunate assumption and it won't happen again, so don't bother to come weaseling back to my bedroom, here or next door, expecting to pick up where you left off. Unless," she amended, reluctant to burn all her bridges with her disastrous propensity for issuing ultimatums, "your intentions undergo an honorable change."

"When hell freezes over," he replied as he closed the door in her face.

CHAPTER ELEVEN

How will I face him? Kim wondered miserably the next morning. How do I sit across the table from him, making small talk and pretending last night didn't happen?

She needn't have worried. The breakfast room adjoining the kitchen was empty, although two places were set. Clearly, she'd beaten Adam downstairs and, with a little luck, could be gone before he was up.

" 'Morning, Ms. Forester." Mrs. Baxter appeared at her elbow, coffeepot in hand. "How do you like your eggs?"

"Good morning, Claudia," she replied. "No eggs, thank you. I only have time for coffee."

"You're not planning to return to the cottage, surely? The Judge won't like that, not until he's had the roof checked out."

"Then the Judge will have to lump it," Kim returned sweetly, adding cream to her coffee, and Mrs. Baxter's jaw sagged. "It's my house. I'll take care of the repairs myself."

The storm had eventually blown itself out about four that morning, but the sky remained solidly overcast. A colorless, depressed sort of day that matched her mood, Kim decided, draining her cup and preparing to leave by the kitchen door. The route through the library was faster, but she was more likely to run into Adam that way. Anyhow, she had to stop by the dog compound for

Muldoon, and it was located around the back of the house.

"Thanks for the coffee," she called out.

"Oh, dear." Sensing something was amiss, Claudia was as close to ruffled as Kim had ever seen her. "Jason will be down in a minute. He and the Judge always eat breakfast together. You'll miss him if you leave now."

"Can't be helped," Kim returned, sliding open the door to the patio. "Tell him I'll see him later." When the Judge isn't around, she added to herself.

It was curiously quiet outside in the wake of last night's violence. A mist was creeping in from the Pacific, damp and clinging, shrouding the trees in tattered gray veils and muting the gentle swish of waves on the shore. Even her footsteps seemed hushed as she followed the path around the house.

His must have been, too, because without warning, Adam emerged from the belt of trees to her right, and short of turning tail and fleeing the other way, Kim had no choice but to acknowledge him. He wore a soft gray fleece jogging suit, a towel tucked at his neck and down inside the front of his kangaroo jacket. He was breathing hard, and Daisy and Muldoon, running at his heels, were panting heavily, their breath forming clouds of vapor in the still air.

Her heart faltered for a second. Adam's hair was dewed with moisture, his skin gleaming, his eyes aloof and watchful. He was beautiful, with his long runner's legs and tapering hips, his solid width and athletic grace, and the pain at having spoiled everything with her impetuous tongue lanced her soul. To have come so close, only to lose it all . . . And she felt in that instant that she couldn't let him go. She'd move mountains to prevent it if she had to.

He spoke first, wiping the dampness from his face with the towel. "You're up early. Looking for Muldoon?"

"Yes."

"I took him with me. He's run about five miles for every one of mine and shouldn't find being penned up in the kennel too painful. He'll probably sleep until noon."

"Actually, I—um—I'm taking him home."

Adam was drying his hair so vigorously that it fell over his forehead in disordered and endearing peaks, making him look younger than his thirty-eight years, but at her words, he lowered his hands and grasped the towel ends as they hung down his chest. "I hope you don't think you're going back to the cottage."

Yesterday, she would have bristled at the implied command. Today, she grasped it as eagerly as a lifeline. Anything was preferable to his indifference. "You don't think I should?"

"Don't be so damn silly, Kim. There's a gaping hole in the roof with a tree lying across it."

She watched the little puffs of his breath hang in the cold air and wanted to lean forward and taste them, inhale them. "I'll call in a repair man—a roofer."

He clicked his tongue impatiently. "You'll stay here until we know the place is safe. Tom has probably already arranged to have someone come out to take a look."

She was to wonder, later, where her temerity came from, but the moment invited an intimacy she couldn't ignore, and without thinking of how he might react, she reached out a hand and placed it over his heart. "If I didn't know better, I'd think you still cared about me."

He shot her an enigmatic glance, cool enough to have deterred her had she not felt the sudden acceleration beneath her fingers. He wasn't as unmoved as he'd like her to believe!

"Don't start on me," he warned her, but she ignored him and stepped closer.

"Then send me away," she murmured, and knew his eyes were lingering on her mouth with a hunger that matched her own. "Tell me you don't want me around, and I'll leave."

"Want you?" he grated, his voice raw and angry. "Damn your beautiful hide, I can't function for wanting you."

He hauled her roughly to him, his unshaven cheek rasping against her soft skin, his lips cold and sweet as a mountain spring. She bent before him, pliant as a willow, welcoming the punishment of his kiss.

"Oh, Adam . . ." she gasped as his lips blazed a trail to her throat. "Oh . . . darling . . ." It was a calculated gamble, the repetition of an endearment she suspected came to neither of them easily. Her words bathed him in tenderness, and with a soft groan, he buried his face in her hair and held her prisoner in his tormented embrace.

"I love you," she whispered, her voice shaking with the painful truth of her words. *"I love you."*

For a second, he was still, then gathering his fraying control, he put her from him. "And where does that leave us?" he inquired in a deceptively mild tone.

"Wherever you want it to." Anything, she wanted to beg. Anything but that chilling disbelief you showed last night.

"Well"—he cleared his throat—"I've made it plain enough that I want you."

Oh, indeed he had. A man could keep few secrets in a fleecy cotton jogging suit. But she wisely refrained from telling him so.

"So," he continued, "I guess the question is whether or not that's enough for you."

She looked at him blankly, her optimism evaporating. "Enough?" she echoed, and felt a flush of outrage race up her neck as the full meaning of his words hit her. "You mean, will I settle for us sleeping together?"

"I prefer the term 'lovers' to 'sleeping together,' " he replied.

"Call it what you like," she seethed. "It all comes

down to the same thing. All you're really interested in is my body."

"Actually, you're wrong," he contradicted her. "I find your devious little mind an endless source of fascination. But I can't deny your body—"

"Sex!" she hissed, and huddled away from him as though to deny the very attributes he found so alluring. "That's what it comes down to: plain, unadulterated lechery!"

He grinned in unabashed amusement. It was role-playing time again, with the deflowered virgin occupying center stage. What next? he wondered, and stepped nimbly aside as she took a swing at his unprotected jaw.

"And you think it's all a big joke, as usual," she flung at him.

"Kim"—he held out a placating hand—"we both know it's there—the chemistry, the attraction, whatever you want to call it. What's the point in denying it?"

"None, I suppose, but I never would have let you make love to me if that was all there was between us. By itself, sex isn't enough."

"And we both know it's more than just sex, so stop with the martyred act."

"It is?" Hope illuminated her face. "Then why are we fighting like this?"

"Because I know how I feel and what prompted my actions. It's your motives that bother me."

"But I've told you, Adam: I love you. And I hoped making love would lead to something . . . deep and lasting."

"You thought it would wring a proposal out of me, Kim—that I'd feel obligated to marry the woman I'd seduced."

"Oh, don't be ridiculous," she retorted. "That sort of thing went out with hobble skirts."

"In that case, there's no real problem, is there? We

agree there's more to our relationship than just sex, so there's no reason we can't go on as we were."

"You mean have an affair?"

"For want of a better expression, yes. For now."

She impaled him with a glare. "When hell freezes over," she mimicked, her voice tight with disappointment. Snapping her fingers for Muldoon to follow, she turned away.

His voice halted her. "It's marriage or nothing, then?"

She stopped and flung him a backward glance. "Exactly. Not just because it's the most conventional or logical resolution, which should appeal to your way of looking at things, but because it's also the most satisfying."

"It would never last, Kim."

"Why not?" She swung back to face him. "Why can't you believe I love you? So what if I love Jason, too? What's so wrong with that?"

"We're wrong—for each other. Oh, I know—" he hastened to add as she opened her mouth to dispute his words. "I know the feelings are there. I also know we'd destroy each other in a relationship as demanding and intimate as marriage. It would be all over inside a year."

"But we belong together," she insisted, her voice breaking on a sob. "How can you ignore what we've got between us?" Huge tears welled in her eyes and overflowed to roll down her cheeks. "Adam . . . please?" She was begging, groveling even, her Forester pride in rags about her feet, and she didn't care.

In a single stride, he closed the space that separated them and hugged her to him. "Oh, honey," he muttered, "don't think I'm not tempted."

"Well then, stop fighting it and give in." She was hanging on to handfuls of his kangaroo jacket and wailing like a child, the tears dripping off her nose and chin and soaking the soft gray fleece.

"Kim"—he shook her gently—"listen to reason."

"No," she sobbed. "I'm sick of reason. It's got nothing to do with loving."

And it was precisely that, Adam thought, that prevented him from piling them both into the car and roaring off to find the nearest minister or justice of the peace. "It has everything to do with it," he insisted. "The courts are filled with people who tried to build a life without it; they're filled with embittered lonely men and women and their broken dreams. I see the children of those marriages every day—lost, neglected, caught in the irreconcilable differences between their parents."

She sniffed and wiped her nose on his towel. "It would be different with us."

"Why?" he demanded, grimacing at the pain in her eyes and in his heart. "Look at the facts: we're polar opposites. I'm logical and realistic; you're impulsive and idealistic. Then there are your reasons for coming out here on the spur of the moment, after months of silence. What prompted it, Kim? Tired of the jet set and ready for something more domesticated?"

He watched the blood drain from her face; he saw her eyes dilate with strange shock before they grew veiled in secrecy. "How long," he asked her, dismayed at the evasion in her flickering glance, "before dissatisfaction eats away again and rubs the bloom off our relationship? A year? Two? Three, before you grow tired of the wifely role, lose heart for the incessant demands of motherhood?"

She tried to turn away so that he wouldn't see the despair that she knew was written all over her face, but he wouldn't let her. He reached out instead and yanked her back to face him. "Well? What will you do then? Yearn for the pace and sophistication of Boston and go back as suddenly as you left, leaving your victims to manage as best they can—me too soured and disillusioned to rebuild my life, and Jason another damaged, abandoned child?"

157

"It would never be like that! I couldn't walk out—"

"You did once. You could do it again. Don't ask me to take that sort of chance."

She sagged with sudden defeat. How could she defend herself without multiplying all his doubts? "You think you've got me all figured out, don't you? But you haven't, not by a long shot. It's nowhere near as uncomplicated as you'd like to believe."

"Really?" His eyes were bleak with disbelief. "Can you honestly say you'd be quite as anxious to formalize our relationship if you hadn't taken such a beating in the custody suit? Wasn't getting even the motive that brought you out here again?"

"You think I want you because that's the only way I can get Jason," she stated dully.

"Let's just say you stand to gain quite a lot by becoming Mrs. Adam Ryan."

She pushed herself away from him. "And stand to lose everything by becoming your mistress: my self-respect, my peace of mind, not to mention my credibility as a surrogate parent. What court would even consider me suitable if I did as you ask?"

"Can't we put the custody suit aside?"

"Apparently not," she replied bitterly. "You bring it up every chance you get. And what do you want instead? To pick up where we left off last night? No, thanks. I'd find it too painful and too compromising. I don't want half a loaf, Adam. I want the whole thing."

This time when she turned away, he made no move to stop her.

Court convened at ten, but by two thirty, when the last case had been heard, Adam felt as though he'd put in an eighteen-hour day.

He shouldn't have been presiding, he knew. His thoughts had wandered from the case before him and drifted repeatedly to the scene with Kim that morning.

158

There had been something he couldn't put his finger on, a subterfuge about her that was out of character. It didn't add up, but then, nothing did. They'd played such games with each other and played them so well that neither one could ever be really sure of the other's good faith. Nor even, he reflected irritably, of their own. Dammit, he'd made the right—the sane—decision for both of them and for Jason. Why did he feel he'd stabbed her in the heart?

He needed to get away, he thought, from the pressures of work and Kim. He was scheduled to fly to the state capital tomorrow to attend a conference on juvenile detention homes. Maybe he'd take a few days off afterward. Go down to San Diego, look up some friends, do a little sailing. Then, when he got back, he'd reassess the situation and hope time and distance would lend him better perspective.

"The repairs must be taken care of today." Kim was adamant. Quite apart from the damage to her furnishings, she would camp out on the beach before she'd spend another night under Adam's roof.

"It'll be a temporary patching job," Rudy Werner told her. "You need new shakes, and with all the rain we've had, I'm not about to send any of my men to work on that steep pitch. It was tough enough bringing that tree down. We'll nail some aluminum sheeting up for now."

"How long before you can do the job properly?"

"After a couple of days of dry weather, preferably with sun. At this time of year, that could be weeks from now."

Good grief! She might just as well pack her stuff and go back to Boston. She'd lost Adam, she'd never be more than a visiting aunt to Jason, and now she didn't even have a place to live. "Okay." She threw up her hands. "Okay! Whatever you say."

She left him to make the temporary repairs and went inside to assess the damage. The bed linen was soaked; the top of the chiffonier was milky with rain spots. Just like her life, it was a disaster area, all the treasured, lovely things in danger of being spoiled by elements beyond her control. And the really disturbing thing was that she no longer cared. She couldn't face the bedspread, not without picturing Adam's tawny limbs stretched out on it. As for the chiffonier—she wanted the solid, comforting warmth of Adam's body next to hers in the night, not the unyielding, inanimate chunk of mahogany that housed her lingerie.

She had nothing to hold on to, she realized. She was a person adrift, seeking an emotional lifeline only to find, each time she thought she'd found it, that it was anchored to nothing of substance. She'd come to the West Coast to forge a continuing link with Greg through his son, only to discover that attachments to family were no substitute for the passionate adult love between a man and a woman.

Even her memories of Greg had shifted, shaded with reality, colored by awareness. They no longer sustained her and had been filed away weeks ago—fond, not-quite-perfect mementos to be taken out and looked at just occasionally. They weren't enough to live her life by anymore. Not since Adam. And his rejection had left a gaping wound in her heart, beside which the hole in her roof was a mere inconvenience. Oh, if only she could be so easily repaired, requiring nothing more than a couple of days of sunshine. And to think she'd once believed she could bring him to his knees with the aid of a plunging neckline.

The telephone by the bed jangled stridently and her hopes soared. If it were Adam calling to coax her, just a little, she might be persuaded to yield, just a little. Her voice lilted with eagerness. "Hello?"

But it was not Adam at the other end; it was Evan, calling from Los Angeles. "Do you have room in that ramshackle cabin for a house guest for a few days?" he asked. "I'm supposed to be making useful contacts at a convention, but the food is atrocious and the smog's even worse."

Diversion came in many shapes, but none was more reassuring than Evan. "For you, always. How soon can you get here?"

"Tomorrow, late afternoon."

"Hurry," Kim said. "Your timing couldn't be better."

Evan arrived four hours after Adam left, and the day after, Claudia came down with bronchitis.

"Of course I'll take Jason," Kim assured Tom over the phone. "Bring him across anytime."

The cottage would be crowded, but at least it left her less time to brood over Adam's absence. Evan was sleeping on the sofabed in the living room, and Jason would share the bedroom with her, but nothing could quite fill the empty ache in her heart. Whatever the reason for his sudden departure, couldn't Adam at least have taken the time to pick up the phone and say good-bye?

"You don't mind, do you?" she asked Evan, explaining the situation to him. "He's really adorable, most of the time."

"Jason or his uncle?" Evan teased her.

She flushed under his searching glance. She had gone on at length about Adam, and Evan was concerned about her, she knew. They'd sat up late the previous evening, talking about her life.

"You mean you flung yourself at his feet and he looked down his long nose and said, 'No, thanks'?" Evan had joked.

"More or less. Isn't he a louse?"

"And a fool."

"A cad."

"An idiot."

"Heartless and—"

"Cold and cruel—"

161

"And I love him."

There was a pause. "And you love him." Evan had lowered his eyes to the glass in his hand, but not quickly enough to hide his dismay from her.

"I do," she assured him. "I really do, Evan."

"He's become your whole life in just a few months. Are you certain you're not repeating past mistakes?"

"You mean looking for a substitute for Greg?" She gave a hollow laugh. "Lord, Evan, there's nothing the least fraternal about my feelings for Adam. Everything would be so much simpler if there were."

"But you may be looking for another idol," he cautioned her. "Someone you can revolve your life around—again. What happens if things don't work out between the two of you? Can you face that?"

Could she? She hadn't been able to answer him, and the question had kept her awake half the night. She'd come too close to collapsing when Greg died and Adam won Jason not to be aware of her fragility in coping with stress or dealing with loss. Yet, there was a conclusiveness about death and, she'd come to see, a certain comfort in the knowledge that its intrusion touched everybody with grief. After a time, sorrow dealt its own healing, and the survivors were swept into the momentum of life, simply because there was no going back to the way things were before.

But rejection—by Adam? She really didn't know if she could handle that. The thought of his leading a separate life, perhaps with another woman to whom he'd make love with the passion and tenderness he'd shown her, was a kind of death in itself, one from which she might never be released. If he should choose to live his life without her, she feared she'd spend the years waiting and hoping that one day he'd see what a fool he'd been and come back to her.

162

* * *

Footsteps on the veranda intruded into her thoughts. "Actually, they're both adorable, but I was referring to Jason," she replied to Evan's question. "See for yourself."

She opened the doors and Jason erupted into the room, babbling nonstop, the reserve he'd once shown her completely gone. "How about a hug?" She swept him into her arms and was rewarded with a throttling embrace.

"Cookies?" he asked hopefully, planting a wet kiss on her cheek.

"After you say hello to Evan and help me put your stuff away." She lowered him to the floor and turned to Tom. "Come in, Tom, and let me take all that. How's Claudia?"

"She'll be better after a couple of days in bed, but—" He stopped as Evan rose from the couch. "Oh, say, Ms. Forester, if I'd known you had company—"

"Don't be silly, Tom. You don't need to be chasing Jason around right now, and Dr. Brewster can use the exercise. Evan, this is Tom Baxter. Dr. Brewster is a very old friend from Boston, Tom."

"Nice to meet you," Evan replied, nodding. "Sorry your wife's not well."

"Thanks." Tom cast a speculative eye on the stranger, then turned to Kim. "You sure this isn't inconvenient? I wouldn't ask, but the Judge won't be back until the beginning of next week."

Seven whole days to go. Oh, misery! "Of course you should ask," she replied briskly. "I'd be offended if you didn't. You know I love having Jason around."

"But all day and night? He's a real going concern, you know."

"Well, I've got Evan if I need help, and I can always phone you if I have problems. You're only next door."

"I suppose." Tom turned away, obviously doubtful about a number of things, not the least of which was

163

Evan's presence in her house. It warmed her heart that in Tom's eyes at least she belonged to Adam.

"You've got yourself a knight in shining armor there," Evan observed as the door closed behind the other man. "He doesn't trust me one little bit."

"He's not the only one," Kim replied, stooping to unpeel Jason's tenacious grip on her leg. "This little guy's not too impressed with you, either."

"Terrific. Another member of the Ryan household bent on defending your honor." Evan approached Jason and squatted down in front of him. "It's okay," he coaxed. "She's in safe hands."

"Go home," Jason ordered, peering at him doubtfully.

"Oh, charming," Evan said, grinning. "Just what you've always wanted, Kim, a protective little ankle-biter. How do I convince him I'm harmless?"

"Slowly," she advised, recalling her own first meeting with Jason.

"Kids his age are usually more outgoing," Evan said. "Come on, Jason. Show me what you've got in the Snoopy bag."

"Mine," Jason warned, reaching out a chubby fist, then seeing Evan looming close, changed his mind and buried his face in Kim's legs again.

"He's got Greg's coloring."

"But not his eyes. He's got Adam's eyes. Isn't he beautiful?" Kim hugged the little body to hers.

"Well . . ." Evan remarked as he went back to his seat on the sofa, "obviously things are working out between the two of you. You're a natural, Kim. Adam's a fool to question your devotion to the child."

"Go home," Jason suggested again, peeking out from behind Kim's knees.

"Not me, pal. I'm sleeping right here, so why don't you come over and get acquainted?" Evan reached down and emptied the bag of toys at his feet. "Hey, take a look at this neat thing."

He poked at the sturdy firetruck on the rug, pushing it back and forth across the floor. It was an inspired move. Jason's Snoopy bag was his constant companion, the repository of his most cherished possessions. He could no more resist its lure than he could ignore the cookie jar.

"I think you're a hit," Kim remarked an hour later.

"I think I am, too," Evan panted. "And I think I like the feeling." Jason had abandoned the truck sometime earlier in favor of the joys and thrills of riding a human, bareback. "I'm also being worn to a shadow. Do rug rats ever run out of energy?" He rolled over and hoisted Jason onto his chest. "What do you say, rug rat?"

"Rug rat," Jason gurgled, and squealed with glee as Evan tossed him up in the air.

"Be careful what you say," Kim warned, laughing. "He's at the age where he repeats everything he hears."

Tom phoned the next day to check on Jason.

"He's fine," Kim assured him. "Don't worry about him. Evan's having the time of his life with him."

"I bet he is," Tom replied darkly. "The Judge called last night."

Did he indeed! "Oh, really?" She feigned indifference. "Give him my best if he calls again. How's Claudia?"

"I told him you were looking after Jason."

And what else did you tell him? she was tempted to ask. "He didn't object, did he?"

"Not that I could tell. Maybe he felt better knowing you had help."

Aha! "Maybe so. Keep me posted on Claudia, Tom."

Adam must be choking on curiosity, to say the least, she reflected, and was not greatly surprised when he cut short his absence and showed up at her door two days later. Evan and Jason had just finished setting up an illuminated tank of tropical fish, the result of a shopping trip to Haida Falls that morning. Jason had his eager little nose pressed to the glass, entranced by the column of rising bubbles and the lazy grace of the black angel fish as they explored their new home.

"And those are neon tetras," Evan pointed out as a school of brilliant shapes darted by.

"Fish," Jason decided, opting for the simple life.

Muldoon, who'd been equally fascinated by the new arrivals, was distracted by some outside noise. Lifting her eyes from the sketching block on her lap, Kim caught sight of Adam prowling along the veranda to the French doors.

"Hello," she sang out, admitting him to the living room and feasting her eyes on his flinty features. "We hadn't expected you back until Monday." Not the exact truth, perhaps, but who was to know?

"I can see that," Adam returned, managing a barely civil nod at Evan. "Am I interrupting something?"

"Not at all. This is Evan Brewster, a very old family friend from Boston. He and Greg were close friends."

Evan extended his hand. "Kim's told me a lot about you."

"Has she?" Adam replied. "That's interesting—because she's never mentioned a word about you . . . until today." And Kim's heart rejoiced at the cold, antagonistic gleam in Adam's eye.

"Kim and I go back a long way." Unperturbed, Evan regarded him with frank curiosity. "How's your housekeeper?"

"Somewhat better."

"Well, that's good news, but I hope it doesn't mean you'll be taking Jason back. We've had a great time together, haven't we, Jason?"

Jason remained glued to the aquarium, supremely indifferent to the subtle hostilities being tossed back and forth between the two men.

Kim reached over and ruffled his hair. "Adam's here, Jason."

"Hi," Jason replied offhandedly, clearly finding the news less than arresting.

Adam's expression darkened forbiddingly and Kim quaked. Enough was enough; she had no wish to push Adam's patience too far. "Say hello properly, Jason." She turned the child firmly toward his uncle. "Aren't you glad to see him?"

"Uh-huh," came the devastating reply. "Go home, 'Dam."

"That seems to be his favorite expression," Kim hastened to explain. "He said the same thing to Evan at first. I'm sure he doesn't mean a thing by it. He's just learning to string words together, that's all."

"You don't need to explain my own child to me," Adam cut in, recovering his poise at the expense of hers. "Just get his bag and clothes. I *am* taking him home." He directed the information at Evan.

"If you feel you must," Evan returned smoothly. "In a way, I should thank you. It gives me more time alone with Kim."

"Having a two-year-old around must have cramped your style, I'm sure."

"No more than it does yours," Evan replied easily.

Adam's nostrils flared dangerously, and Kim paled. A little competitive jealousy was healthy, but full-fledged war she could do without. "We've loved having him, Adam."

"Oh, spare me," he jeered. "He must have upset your plans no end."

"What plans?"

"To entertain your . . . friend . . . the minute my back was turned."

Kim gasped. "That's absurd. I didn't even know you were going out of town until the day you left."

"Didn't waste much time, once you found out, did you?"

"Hey!" Evan stepped between them. "Enough of the sleazy insinuations. What sort of man are you, anyway?"

"About three inches taller and thirty pounds heavier than you," Adam shot back, and Kim could not repress the amusement that suddenly consumed her at the sight of her cool, poised Adam glaring truculently at the one man he had no reason to resent.

"Gentlemen, please. Not in front of Jason." She eyed Adam surreptitiously. Where had he been to acquire that tanned glow? Evan looked positively washed out by comparison. "Why don't we all sit down and have a drink, and you can tell us about your trip."

"I'll pour," Evan offered amicably. "What'll you have, Ryan?"

"Bourbon," Adam replied shortly, steering Kim to the couch and seating himself firmly next to her.

Oh, he was precious when he was possessive! She basked in his indignant attention. "We've missed you," she murmured.

For a moment, his gaze softened. "Have you?"

"But we managed," Evan interjected, thrusting a tumbler into Adam's hand. "And I think we made out pretty well, all things considered."

Made out? Adam contained himself with difficulty. *Made out?*

Sensing he was nearing flash point, Kim rested her hand placatingly on his knee and was shocked at the tension that communicated itself to her. "Jason was rather shy with Evan at first," she explained hurriedly. "It took him a while to accept a stranger, but they're great friends now."

Adam drained his glass. "Let's hope he doesn't find the parting too painful, then." Abruptly, he rose to his feet and strode over to Jason. "Time to go home, sport."

He went to hoist the child to his shoulders, but Jason had other ideas. "Down!" he bellowed, outraged at being dragged away from the fish tank.

"Sorry, Jason, but we have to go. You can come back tomorrow and visit some more."

"No!" Jason roared in protest, kicking wildly at Adam's midriff.

"That's enough," Adam reproved him sharply. "Behave yourself."

Jason wriggled out of his uncle's grip. "No," he repeated defiantly, his lower lip trembling ominously.

"He's tired, Adam. He and Evan spent the day shopping, and he didn't get his nap."

"My fault, I'm afraid," Evan added. "Perhaps we should have waited until later to set up the tank."

Adam reached again for his nephew, visibly reining in his temper. "All the more reason to get him home and to bed now, then. Come along, son."

But Jason was not disposed to be cooperative. "No," he wept, running to where Kim still sat on the couch. "Rug rat!" he shot at his astonished uncle, then buried his face in her lap, at which Evan got up and discreetly left the room.

CHAPTER TWELVE

Adam could scarcely credit the rage that shook him. Jason's little tantrum, by itself, he could handle. But the sight of Evan Brewster, calmly disappearing into Kim's kitchen and obviously very much at home there if the rattle of pots and pans was any indication, inflamed in him a hitherto unsuspected streak of jealousy that verged on violence. To know that with very little provocation he would happily plant his foot in the seat of Brewster's pants and evict him from the premises was shocking.

So much for putting a little distance between Kim and himself. He'd failed so miserably to banish her from his thoughts that he'd almost welcomed the excuse to return home early at the news of the interloper's arrival—until he was confronted with the evidence of a relationship that had clearly weathered the test of time. They were so bloody comfortable with each other!

He hated himself—almost hated her—for the tormenting suspicions growing in his mind. Where had Brewster slept the past few nights?

The image of Kim's golden body exposed to another man's poaching paws clawed at him. No point in calling on reason. Until recently his most dependable asset in dealing with women, it had repeatedly failed to extricate him from the powerful tide of passion he felt for Kim. No use telling himself he had been her only lover. He had been the first, that was all. She had, after all, offered herself to him in marriage, and he'd turned her down brutally. Who knew what measures she might take to repair her battered pride? Hell hath no fury . . . he reminded himself grimly.

The urge to grasp her in both hands and shake a confession from her was a fever in his blood. By God, if she'd let Brewster lay so much as a finger on her, he'd not be responsible for his actions.

"Couldn't he have stayed in a hotel or something?"

She was coaxing Jason into his jacket and stopped briefly to return Adam's furious glare with a mildly inquiring glance. "Why should he? There's room enough here, and the nearest hotel is twelve miles down the highway."

The jealousy coiled through him. Brazen hussy, he seethed. Unclenching his fists, he turned again to Kim, his gaze as deadly as the steely lash of his tongue. "Get Jason's bag," he ordered, *"now."*

She opened her mouth to protest, and at the sight of her parted lips, he experienced a blinding urge to sink his mouth to hers and pillage its ruby depths. Dammit, he suddenly wanted her so badly that he ached.

Then she bit down gently on her lip, depriving him of the erotic vision of her tongue sliding moistly over her smooth and shining teeth, and the predatory hunger that had swamped him receded. He shook his head, dazed and weary. Was he going mad?

"I think we let things go too far," Kim confided to Evan after Adam and Jason had left.

"I think the good judge is a sight more enamored of you than he'd like to believe," Evan rejoined. "Eat your fettuccine."

"I'm not hungry." She pushed her plate aside. "I think he was very angry."

"Shocked," Evan corrected her, "as much by his own response as anything. But he'll get over it, and a lot sooner if I move out of the picture, so I'll hit the road

171

tomorrow. It's time I got back, in any case. I have people waiting for my help—and you, my love, aren't one of them."

"No," she said, and propping her elbow on the table, sank her chin to her fist, "not anymore."

"A suggestion . . . ?"

She looked up and caught him observing her closely. "What?"

"Tell Adam about your minor depressive episode."

Her eyes flew wide. "Tell him? Are you crazy?"

"No." He smiled. "More to the point, neither are you —nor ever were you."

"Can you imagine how he'd react to such news?" The prospect almost made her heart stop.

"I don't think he'll give a damn, at least not in the way you fear. And you'll feel a whole lot better if you get it out in the open. After all, it's got to come out sooner or later if there's any sort of future for the two of you."

He reached over and covered her hand. "I had a lot of doubts about him," he admitted. "And I mean *a lot*. I was afraid you were setting yourself up for another fall."

"And now?"

"He's okay, his caveman instincts notwithstanding." Evan grinned suddenly. "For an improvisation, I thought my performance was magnificent, but I wondered if I'd overplayed my hand in arousing his possessive instincts. I know I couldn't fight him, but I'm not sure I could out-run him, either." He regarded her seriously. "You *do* know that he loves you?"

"I want to believe it, more than anything."

"Trust me. I know grand passion when I see it—and chemistry." He rose and pushed back his chair. "I'm going to pack. Consider yourself officially discharged."

She smiled up at him. "Thanks, Evan. You're the best friend I ever had."

"Tell me that again when you see my bill," he said, his mouth lifting in a smile that didn't quite reach his eyes.

172

And while the doctor regarded her approvingly, the man looked at her with regretful finality and said his private good-byes.

Evan left in the afternoon, as planned.

Even as she waved her farewells as the taxi sped away, the wheels were turning in Kim's head. She'd follow his advice, she decided. Now, today, before she lost her courage, she'd tell Adam why she'd taken so long to come to Jason.

She closed the front door with resolve and immediately made her way to the phone. "Will you stop by this evening?" she asked when he answered. "There's something I want to discuss."

"What time?"

His tone scarcely augured well, but her foolish heart soared. At least he hadn't refused her. "Nine o'clock?"

She tried to organize her thoughts, to fortify herself to withstand his reactions, whatever they may be. She was sharing an experience with him, that was all. Being as honest as he'd be with her in the same situation. This was neither a shameful secret nor a continuing problem. But her palms were damp, and she dreaded the ordeal ahead.

He arrived early, handsome as sin and surly as the devil. Refusing to let his grim expression deter her, she greeted him with a smile. The tight-lipped salutation she received in return boded ill for a satisfying resolution of their differences, and all she wanted was to smooth the lines of ill temper from his face. He was magnificently formidable in his narrow black cords and high-necked sweater, foul mood or not.

"Would you care for something—coffee, brandy? A liqueur, perhaps?"

He loomed before the fire, a darkly disapproving figure, every erect inch of him radiating displeasure. Ignoring her question, he raked his gaze over the room. "Where's what's-his-name?"

173

Astonished, she stared at his glowering expression. "You mean Evan?"

"Who else? Or are there others waiting in the wings for their turn at a little action?"

"Oh!" she gasped. He could be the most blatantly unpleasant creature when the mood took him. "Honestly, Adam, not everyone has designs on my virtue. Some people, believe it or not, actually revere me for my mind."

"Damn fools," he muttered rudely, then swung back to skewer her with that familiar accusatory glare. "So, where is he?"

"He left this afternoon."

"How interesting. I hope he didn't cut things short on my account."

"He didn't," she snapped. "Difficult though it may be for you to accept, the sun doesn't rise and set for everybody according to your doings." She heaved a suddenly despondent sigh. "Just for me."

She was unquestionably the most foolish woman alive, flagellating herself in this fashion. The man was indomitable. He'd never concede to weakness; he would never understand hers.

"Is *that* what you wanted to talk about—your unflagging devotion to me?" His voice was laced with sarcasm. "How much you missed me? How you were so destroyed by my absence that you had to call in cocky little Brewster-the-Rooster to support you in your lonely grief? What is he, some sort of emotional crutch for the idle rich?"

She could scarcely believe her ears. Brewster-the-Rooster? She blanched, recoiling before his evil glare. "What's the matter with you?" she breathed, awed. She'd never before witnessed such rage in anyone. It sent little tremors of apprehension skating over her skin. And his remark about Evan, though cruelly phrased, was unnervingly accurate. It was the perfect opening for what she wanted to say.

174

Adam took a step toward her, and for a brief second, she half feared and half hoped he might touch her. "Stop it!" he thundered instead, almost jolting her out of her shoes. "Stop the wide-eyed gaze, the innocent 'who-me?' act. Stop the damn games. I'm sick and tired of them. The man's obviously your lover. I saw the way he looked at you. Or was he imported for the sole purpose of bringing me to my knees?"

"He's my friend," she gasped, growing anger contributing to her pallor. "How *dare* you suggest otherwise!"

"Who conveniently shows up the day I leave. And stays here with you. For a woman obsessed with appearances, you showed precious little regard for your reputation." He stopped and drew an irate breath. "Even less for Jason."

"Oh, for heaven's sake, Adam!" She shook her head in disbelief. "Are you suggesting we corrupted Jason's morals?"

"No," he retorted, "because he's too young to know or care what's going on around him as long as he's fed and cared for. But you knew exactly how I'd feel having him exposed to one of Greg Forester's cronies."

"Leave Greg out of this. He's dead, for God's sake. And Evan is a decent, responsible, caring human being. I've learned to let go all the unhappiness of the past. Why can't you?"

"I did," he replied cuttingly. "Then you showed up and brought it all back."

"How? How have I done that? I love Jason—you know I do—and I've tried every way I know how to show you I love you, too."

"By having another man live here behind my back? Couldn't you have found a more conventional way to do it?"

At that, she quite forgot herself. "Oh, stuff convention! And stuff you, too, for that matter."

"Precisely my point, my darling. The Forester ethic in a nut shell."

He was the most hateful snake ever to slither the face of the earth, she decided. Lifting her eyes, she gazed at him coolly. "Jason is a Forester," she reminded him levelly. "You can play Big Daddy all you like, but he is Greg's son. You owe my brother a lot, when you come right down to it. He gave you your reason for living in Jason—poor little thing."

He remained unfazed by her feeble attempt to disconcert him. "And what's your reason for living, Kim? Playing fast and loose with every man who crosses your path? Playing one off against another? Playing—notice how often the word comes up when we talk about you?"

Suddenly she was exhausted with the whole subject, and more than a little disgusted. Had their fine and glorious passion come to this? A mudslinging exchange that robbed even the memories of all their haunting beauty?

She sank down to the chair beside the fire and shrugged her shoulders eloquently. She would not explain to him her temporary living arrangements with Evan—who slept where, and with whom. If Adam's opinion of her was so firmly entrenched in the gutter, there was no point. "All right, Adam, you win. You don't want to believe in me—or in us. You accuse me of being unconventional, but I'm the one who wants marriage over an affair. You won't let me share your life with Jason, no matter how much we all might benefit from doing so. You won't let yourself be happy."

She ran a defeated hand through her hair. "I feel sorry for you," she went on. "The only things you can focus on are other people's past mistakes and disasters. They sour your whole outlook—which is really ironical, all things considered. It was you, after all, who showed me how to put Greg behind me and get on with my life. You who set me free so that I could know the true meaning of being a woman. Why in the world did you go to so much trouble for a tramp?"

His voice was raw with pain. "I never said you were that."

"Sure you did." A chilling disdain crept into her eyes. "You think I slept with Evan when your back was turned. We're about as far apart as two people can get. I should have listened to you from the first—or remembered what Greg told me about you. Either way, I never would have become involved with you."

Adam laughed shortly. "Greg was hardly in a position to criticize anyone else, considering the way he behaved."

"His behavior stacks up pretty well beside yours. At least he was prepared to offer Jocelyn marriage. In any case, he was my brother and I won't keep apologizing for his shortcomings, or for mine. You want to believe I slept with Evan, so be my guest. I just wish I'd thought of it first."

There was a moment of utter silence during which his gaze punctured her bubble of defiance until it hung in shreds, and all she wanted to do was crawl under her chair and hide her head in shame. Then, seeming to have looked at her soul and read the infamy there, he turned away and let himself out the door with ominous restraint.

Things, Kim reflected morosely as she watched the latest in a series of weather fronts stream down her dining room windows, could hardly be worse. At this rate, spring—and she, perhaps—would be come and gone before the roof was properly repaired. As for her heart, she had little hope that it would ever mend.

It had been three days since the disastrous meeting with Adam. Almost seventy-two hours in which to replay and regret and repent, and nothing could diminish the enormity of the breach they'd created between them. The pain of it hounded her night and day.

She turned listlessly from the rain-swept seascape at

the pounding on the kitchen door. "Go away," she begged quietly, but she found herself answering the summons, completely indifferent to who might be there and why their knocking should be so intrusive. That was, until she saw through the window that Adam waited outside, grasping Muldoon by the collar, and then giddy hope swamped her.

"Hello." Her smile was a ray of bright sunshine in the dark day. "Where did you find him?"

Muldoon was soaked and muddy, and Adam, she noticed with resignation, was pale with anger. "Take your precious dog," he snapped, "and keep him confined to his own property."

"What did he do, Adam?" she inquired sweetly. "Fertilize your rose bed?"

"That would be bad enough."

Something about Adam's tone gave Kim pause, and she examined Muldoon more closely. Oh, no! He had a philandering, exhausted, sated look to him that she recognized.

"He fertilized my purebred shepherd," Adam snarled.

Quite unable to help herself, Kim erupted into helpless giggles. "Oh," she managed to gasp, "what a relief. If he'd bitten you, he'd have needed a rabies shot—for his own protection."

The dog yelped in pained protest as Adam hauled him into the kitchen and shoved the door closed with his shoulder. "If that's not typical," he blazed. "Only a Forester would be so bloody irresponsible. What about my dog?"

"She probably had the time of her life," Kim chortled. "Muldoon's quite a lady's man." She leaned weakly against the marble counter, her merriment edging a little closer to shrill hysteria. Another lusty and unscrupulous Forester had seduced a Ryan maiden!

Who would get custody? she wondered wildly. Or would there be enough furry little bundles of joy to keep

178

everyone satisfied? Her laughter ricocheted off the walls, but she couldn't see Adam's anger dissolve into concern because the tears were flooding her eyes and washing down her cheeks.

"Kim!" His hands were urgent in their restraint, his voice rough with remorse. He shook her and her head lolled like a doll's with a broken neck. "Get a hold on yourself," he begged.

"I can't," she wailed. "I'm mentally unhinged—can't you tell? Nutty as a fruitcake. Ask Dr. Brewster-the-Rooster. He has all the details."

She wanted to slip between the smooth ceramic tiles of the floor, into the dark safety of the earth below. But Adam wouldn't let her go, for all that she let her bones relax until they seemed insubstantial as air. He wrapped her in his arms, instead, and Muldoon, naughty, lecherous Muldoon, pressed his head against her knees in silent sympathy. And between them, they held on to her until the world righted itself again and the tears ran dry.

"Why do I cry so much around you?" she finally asked, and hiccupped gently.

"Oh, darling," Adam whispered, and the tenderness was back in his voice, the love in his eyes—and all just a fraction too late to forestall the outrage that suddenly consumed her.

Why was it that he always waited until she had her back to the wall before he volunteered his love and concern? Was that his way of punishing her for her past omissions and errors? His way of pointing up her inferiority, not just in the matter of Jason's custody but in her right to a man's love and tenderness? Damn him, he had no right, no right at all, to set himself up as her judge.

"Don't 'darling' me," she whispered in quiet fury, the tears drying on her cheeks. "Save it for someone more worthy, because, God knows, I'll never measure up to your impossible expectations. And you know what? I

179

don't want to try anymore." She was a tigress in her rage, her amber eyes glowing like fire.

"You don't mean that." He tried to wrap her in his arms again, but she backed away, her hand upraised to ward him off.

"Oh, yes, I do. I've tried to do my part, but it just never occurred to you that you had to do yours, too, and I'm not interested in a one-way relationship. Now, get out of my house and leave me alone."

Reaching into a drawer, she hauled out one of Muldoon's towels, and taking the dog by the collar, she turned her back on Adam and left him standing in the middle of the kitchen. She was on her knees before the fire, drying off her dog, before she heard the outside door close.

He had gone, then—taken her at her word and left without making a last attempt to set things right. The giving always had to come from her, she acknowledged bitterly, then steeled herself to withstand the barbs of pain that assaulted her.

Dispirited beyond words, she leaned her back against the couch and stretched out her toes to the warmth of the flames in the hearth. Immediately, Muldoon lay down beside her and rested his head in her lap.

Absently, she fondled his silky ears and let the peace and quiet of the room sift through her. Gradually, the thoughts that had whirled through her mind like the flying colors of a kaleidoscope fell into a settled design, and she saw how things were now, and what she must do.

She was alone—except for Muldoon. Alone and coping. She'd made mistakes, some of them horrendous, but none, she realized with dawning hope, that she could not forgive. Because whatever her shortcomings, she'd grown over the last six months, as a person and as a woman.

She was still imperfect—she always would be—but that didn't diminish her worth as a human being. She couldn't erase the past, but she could—and must—set herself a different pattern for the future. It took courage to be grown up, and strength and responsibility, and she felt suddenly confident that she had developed enough of all three to face the future on her own.

Oh, yes, she admitted, her eyes misting with tears, she did love Adam. But what she wanted from him was his acceptance of her as she was, not his protection or his patronage. She wasn't looking for a crutch anymore. If there was to be a man in her life, he could not be expected to give her self-esteem or even happiness. That had to be her task. His role, she recognized with unsuspected insight, was to be her complementary partner, not her other half. She was complete all by herself.

She must tell Adam about her past, confront him with the reality of her experience, and let him make the choice. He could take her or leave her as he saw fit, but it would be his decision based on a full knowledge of who she had been and what she had become. And if he chose to cut her out of his life, she would go on without him. She would not play Victorian heroine to his massive ego and let him become her raison d'être.

Accepting, exhausted, she curled up on the couch, her knees drawn up under her, and rested her head on the cushioned arm. She had just fought—and won—a major battle.

Adam found her there, coming to her as silently as afternoon slid into evening. She looked up from her half sleep, and he was there, watching her out of concerned gray eyes.

"The fire's almost out and you're cold," he said, reaching for the crocheted shawl flung over the sofa back. "Let me cover you, then I'll bring in more wood."

She could have borne anything but his kindness. Anger, scorn, rejection—she was armed against them all. But his gentle hands and his warm voice destroyed her utterly. Her face crumpled along with her composure and she sagged against him. "There is something I have to tell you," she said miserably before her courage deserted her completely. "Something about me."

"Me first," he broke in. "Before you say a word, I've got to tell you how sorry I am for the way I've behaved. My only excuse is that I've been half crazy with jealousy."

He perched beside her. "I know there wasn't anything between you and Evan."

"But there was," she replied softly. "He's more than just a friend. That's what I have to tell you."

"Then I don't want to hear about it."

There was a wealth of pain in his tone, a world of agony in his eyes, that unlocked her lips faster than any word of censure could have. "He's a practicing psychiatrist," she said. "And I was his patient for several weeks."

Adam grew very still at that. "Tell me," he urged. "I'm listening."

"The custody battle—it was the last straw. I fell to pieces. You must have sensed something was wrong, the way I acted that day in court. Evan rescued me. He was the only person who knew what was happening to me, the only one who understood what losing Greg had done to me."

"Yes," Adam nodded. "You were pretty unstrung that day, but I thought it was because you'd lost Jason."

She passed a hand over her eyes, as though to dispel the wretched memories. "Well, in a way, it was. But I didn't want him just to spite you. I wanted him to take Greg's place."

"That would have been impossible."

"And unfair. I know that now. But at the time, I hurt so badly that all I could think was that if Jason were with me, there'd be someone there that I could hold on to during the night. And for a little while, I was afraid it

182

would always be night for me, even when the sun was up. I didn't think there would ever be daylight again."

Her suffering reached out and engulfed him. Lord, if he'd only realized . . .

"I hadn't learned then that no one can—no one should have to—stand in for another person. I didn't see how unfair it was to lay all that responsibility on another person's shoulders. I just needed someone, and Jason . . ." She swallowed her tears. "Jason was small and dependent. He needed someone, too."

Adam reached forward and held both her hands. He hated the pale, drawn look that painted violet shadows under her eyes and robbed her face of its sparkling vitality. "Children don't stay dependent for ever, though," he pointed out softly. "They grow up, faster than we'd like."

"I know," she admitted. "But at the time, I didn't consider that—or think of what was best for Jason. You were right to doubt my motives."

"If I'd known—"

"I was a mess," she continued determinedly. "It was weeks before I stopped running away from all that had happened and saw things in some sort of perspective. That's why I didn't come out here sooner. It wasn't because I was sulking or too busy partying to be bothered. I just wouldn't have been good for Jason. A child needs someone he can rely on. He was better off with you, then."

Her grief reached out and closed around his heart in a painful fist. "But now he needs both of us," he told her. "He's not looking for perfection or keeping track of our mistakes. He knows we love him, and that's all that matters to him."

"You don't understand. I'm not always strong like you. Sometimes I do stupid, thoughtless things. I've been irresponsible and deceitful and manipulative—everything you've ever said I was. All these months, I've been hiding this from you, and heaven knows how much longer I'd have gone on doing it if things hadn't come to a head today."

"Kim." Her words stung his eyes with near-forgotten tears. Here she'd been fighting uphill all along, and all he'd ever done was systematically tear her down every time she tried to prove herself to him.

How could he have been such a jackass? he wondered bitterly. Any fool knew better than to treat a thorough-bred racing animal like a common plow horse, yet he'd handled his beautiful, spirited Kim with all the finesse of a ham-fisted blacksmith. Had he broken her with his repeated attacks on her integrity?

"You have to know what I'm really like, before we let our relationship go any further."

He pulled her to him and held her cold, despairing body against the steady pulsing warmth of his heart. "I know what you're like," he said hoarsely. "And I love you. Oh, darling, I do. And so does Jason."

That crack in the dam of her emotions, the one she'd been so hard-pressed to contain, tore apart at his words and let the final truth spill through in a flood of new tears. "No, you don't know," she sobbed. "I used you. I planned to make you fall in love with me so that I could get Jason."

He rocked her in his arms, patiently waiting until the rush of tears exhausted itself. "Are you saying," he asked finally, "that it's all been an act? That you don't really love me, after all?"

She turned her rain-washed eyes up to his face and let them linger on each beloved feature. "Oh," she sighed on a long, shuddering inhalation, "I love you more than I ever knew I could love anyone. But at first—"

"You resorted to witchcraft," he teased, "with a black silk dress as tempting as sin instead of a cloak and a pointed hat, and a crazy Irish setter instead of a cat. Did you think you had me fooled?"

"I didn't think at all. I just felt."

"And I," he said, drawing her head to his shoulder, "did altogether too much thinking."

The logs shifted in the hearth, shooting sparks up the chimney, the flames weaving hypnotic spells that tugged her lashes down to settle in lustrous, gold-tipped fans on her cheeks.

She had a talent for embracing all that was positive and golden in life, he thought. She was early summer, ripe with the promise of fulfillment. And he, in his earnest pursuit of duty, was late autumn—gray, dark, depressing. How could he expect her to forgive him for his blindness? He'd only just learned to forgive himself, to recognize that what had happened to Jocelyn was over and that it was the future with Jason—and, he prayed, with Kim—that mattered now.

He watched the tension melt from her face and thought she was sleeping. Carefully, he stole out to the porch and brought in more logs to heap on the fire. Had he ever been that gloriously young? Had he ever possessed the spark that gave life to her mind and illuminated her soul with such a zest for living? At that moment, he felt he'd been born middle-aged and realized that her vitality and the youthful joy that overlaid her womanliness were two of the things he loved most about her.

She stirred in the cocoon of warmth that owed more to the beat of Adam's heart beneath her hand than to the heat from the fire or the cover on her legs. It was still raining outside.

"Is it late?" she asked drowsily.

"Not too late, I hope." His voice rumbled down into his chest and vibrated against the delicate chamber of her ear.

She sat up, sudden anxiety clouding her eyes. "Why do you say that? Has something happened?"

"Nothing," he was quick to assure her, "that you need

185

to worry about. I'm talking about us." She was rosy from sleep and as wide-eyed as a child, but her silk shirt clung to her breasts, stealing his gaze with its subtle shiftings.

"Us?" she echoed softly.

"As in you and me." He let his eyes rediscover her; he let them drift at leisure over the golden cream of her skin, the gentle hollows created, surely, to accommodate his lean angles.

She stared at him, perplexed. "But you said—"

He gently placed a finger over her lips, then let it trail across her cheek until he could slide his hand around her neck and imprison her head. "I know it's asking too much to forget all the things I've said, but please," he begged huskily, "don't remind me what a complete fool I've been."

"You're not angry?"

"Ashamed," he replied, "of myself."

"But there's been so much. First Greg, then all the things I've done. Even Muldoon—"

"And please," he groaned, leaning his forehead on hers, "don't remind me that the dog's got more sense than I have. Don't you see? None of those things have anything at all to do with you and me."

She stirred restively against him. "There's my . . . breakdown and my conniving—"

"There's nothing," he contradicted her, his mouth searching for hers. "There's only you and me, and I've been too blind to see that that's what really counts." His eyes begged her to believe him as his lips caught hers again, fleeting and tender. "Marry me," he murmured against her mouth.

"Oh!" She let out a soft wail. "Oh, I can't. I've decided to be independent."

"Of course you can." He drew her firmly to him. "You can have your independence and still be my wife. I have it on the best possible authority."

"No, Adam. You don't know . . ."

He folded her to his heart and held her there unrelentingly. "I know everything that matters," he insisted soothingly. "I know you're sensitive and loving and loyal. I know I love you and—"

He stopped, stricken, and stared into the infinite golden depths of her beautiful eyes. "Do you still love me?"

That he should even ask! "I can't seem to help myself," she whispered, her soul at last allowing itself to stir with hope. "I must be crazy."

"Not you, despite the cause we all give you." He ran his fingers up her arms and clasped her lightly about the shoulders. "Marry me," he begged again, his glowing gray eyes urgent. "Be my wife, and Jason's mommy, and have my babies, too. There are an old carved cradle and rocking chair in my basement that my grandfather made for my grandmother when they first settled out here. I'll even throw them in as added inducement."

"But why? What's made you change your mind?" With the tips of her fingers, she could define each smooth ridge of muscle beneath the fine wool sweater.

He was drawing her closer, entrapping her with the sorcery of his hands and mouth. "I won't settle for some hole-in-the-corner affair. I love you too much to make do with half a loaf, you minx. What do you think you're doing?"

"Undressing you," she informed him demurely, slipping her smooth, soft hands under his sweater and stroking the lovely, warm planes of his chest. "I don't seem able to help myself."

"I know what you mean," he replied, and tugged her blouse away from her slacks. "Which is another reason we should get married—to make all this groping around legal and respectable. Marriage, after all, is an honorable estate, and I," he rumbled, his body in an uproar of desire, "am nothing if not an honorable man."

"In that case, I suppose I might as well say yes." His

skin was like silk, she marveled, pulling the sweater over his head and feasting her eyes on the sleekly muscled contours of him. "You'll make a beautiful bridegroom."

"Wanton," he groaned, and showered her face with tiny kisses until he found her mouth.

"Oh, darling," she gasped in that special way of hers as his hands curved around the womanly wonder of her.

Muldoon sighed in his sleep and rolled over on the antique Oriental rug, stretching his elegant pedigreed limbs and thrashing his tail in remembered ecstasy. It had been one hell of a day!

ROBERTA GELLIS

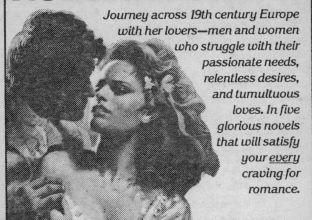

Journey across 19th century Europe with her lovers—men and women who struggle with their passionate needs, relentless desires, and tumultuous loves. In five glorious novels that will satisfy your every craving for romance.

____THE ENGLISH HEIRESS 12141-8-14	**$2.50**
____THE KENT HEIRESS 14537-6-12	**3.50**
____FORTUNE'S BRIDE 12685-1-24	**3.50**
____A WOMAN'S ESTATE 19749-X-23	**3.95**

At your local bookstore or use this handy coupon for ordering:

DELL READERS SERVICE—DEPT. B1226A
P.O. BOX 1000, PINE BROOK, N.J. 07058

Please send me the above title(s). I am enclosing $_____ (please add 75¢ per copy to cover postage and handling). Send check or money order—no cash or COQs. Please allow 3-4 weeks for shipment.
CANADIAN ORDERS: please submit in U.S. dollars.

Ms./Mrs./Mr._____

Address_____

City/State_____ Zip_____

You're invited to a reunion well worth attending

College classmates Emily, Chris, Daphne, and Annabel will be there. Friends from their days at Radcliffe in the 50s, they found glamorous careers, married "perfect" men, and expected to have "perfect" children. They played by the rules —sort of—but the rules changed midway through their lives.

You'll meet them first in Rona Jaffe's wonderful **Class Reunion**. And catch up with these remarkable women 25 years after graduation in **After the Reunion**.

R o n a   J a f f e

_____	CLASS REUNION	11288-5-43	$4.50
_____	AFTER THE REUNION	10047-X-13	4.50

At your local bookstore or use this handy coupon for ordering:

DELL READERS SERVICE—DEPT. B1226B
P.O. BOX 1000, PINE BROOK, N.J. 07058

Please send me the above title(s). I am enclosing $_____(please add 75c per copy to cover postage and handling). Send check or money order—no cash or CODs. Please allow 3-4 weeks for shipment. CANADIAN ORDERS: please submit in U.S. dollars.

Ms Mrs Mr _____

Address_____

City State_____ Zip _____